Bayou
Fever

To the amazing prayer warriors at FOTW, Seared Hearts, and all the others who prayed this book into existence, and to my heavenly Father, who gave me the words when I had none. Also many thanks to Colleen, Aly, and Jan for the meals. I owe you this book and more. God bless you all *et merci bien!*

A note from the Author:
I love to hear from my readers! You may correspond with me by writing:

Kathleen Y'Barbo
Author Relations
PO Box 719
Uhrichsville, OH 44683

ISBN 1-59310-054-X

BAYOU FEVER

Our mission is to publish and distribute inspirational products offering exceptional value and biblical encouragement to the masses.

All Scripture quotations are taken from the King James Version of the Bible.

All of the characters and events in this book are fictitious. Any resemblance to actual persons, living or dead, or to actual events is purely coincidental.

PRINTED IN THE U.S.A.

one

Sweat poured off Angeline Breaux's back and dampened the dress beneath her rough cotton apron as she worked to finish the morning's wash. If only her troubles could be so easily shed. Today Papa would return from town, and he promised to cast off the burden of her care by fetching a husband.

She knew all about husbands. They expected meals on the table and young 'uns in the crib, each replacing the next with a speed that would make the pollywogs in the bayou look slow.

Allowing the Lord to take His time with a match for her had worn her father's patience thin, and Theophile Breaux had sworn to take the matter into his own hands. After all, she'd made twenty years plus one, and her finger still bore no man's ring.

She would be married by fall or to the convent she would go, he declared, even though the Breaux family hadn't professed the religion of the nuns for three generations. Still, Papa had promised as much last Monday morning when he lit out for town with a dugout canoe full of skins and her eldest brother Ernest, and she believed him.

Papa was a good man, but his ways weren't always gentle-hearted. Should he find someone willing to claim his daughter in marriage, he might be more pleased than particular, especially since he would have one less mouth to feed.

If only *Le Bon Dieu* hadn't sent away the one man who. . .

Angeline shrugged off the thought with a roll of her

5

shoulders. Theirs had not been love, and he had certainly not been a man. Children, both of them, and so young and stupid.

If God had a plan for her, He could begin by bringing her a husband.

One thing was for sure. He needed to hurry.

"Angie?"

She looked past the thicket to where her nine-year-old sister Amalie stood watching. "What is it, *Bebe?*" she called. "Does Mama need me?"

"No, I just wanted to watch."

Amalie picked her way through the tall grass to sit at Angeline's side. One of her dark braids had come undone, and Angeline dried her hands on her apron and repaired the mess.

Her sister looked a bit flushed and her hair curled in damp tendrils at her temples. It might be the heat, but Angeline worried it could be the illness that had been lingering nearly a week. One day she would feel fine, the next she seemed weak. It was all so confusing and worrisome, but today she looked to be merely tired.

Scooting as close as she could to the edge of the bayou, the little girl dipped her toes into the water and began to kick. "Mama went visitin', and Mathilde told me I had to take a nap with the babies on account of I've been sick. I told her you probably needed me."

She cast a glance over her shoulder at her sister. "And what did she say to that?"

"Don't know. I didn't wait to hear. I figure the washing's more fun."

Angeline chuckled. "It isn't nearly as much fun as it looks."

"You make everything fun, Angie."

"Well, I don't know about that, but I try." She paused. "So, are you feeling better?"

"Sure, I'm all better." She picked at a nearby leaf and stifled a yawn. "Why don't you tell me a story?"

"You know all my stories," Angeline said. "Why don't you go ask Mathilde to tell you one?"

"I like yours better than Mathilde's, and she doesn't know the one about T-Boy the gator, and that's my favorite." She paused to rub her eyes. "Besides, you don't tell me what to do all the time and she does. If she tells me a story, she'll make me do some chores."

An image of Mathilde, soon to be seventeen and already wanting a husband and babies of her own, came to mind. Poor Amalie probably had a list of instructions a yard long. Mathilde generally kept things orderly and employed an army of brothers and sisters to do the work when she could get away with it.

"I suppose she can be bossy, can't she?"

With a reassuring smile, Angeline went back to her washing. A few minutes later, she noticed Amalie yawning again. The pink in her cheeks had deepened.

"Maybe you'd like to take that old sheet over there and lie down to have a little nap."

Amalie frowned. "You wouldn't make me, would you?"

"I would."

"Well, I'd rather go swimming."

"That's not going to happen, Amalie." She stifled a smile at the girl's audacity. "Now march yourself over there and take your nap before I have to get even more bossy than Mathilde."

Her sister stood. "If I'm gonna have to take a nap, I might as well sleep in a bed. Thanks a lot, Angie." The little girl stormed off, leaving silence in her wake.

❧

Technically, Jefferson Davis Villare was on vacation, although he could think of a half dozen places he'd rather be. Actually, he had no more choice in the matter of visiting the bayou one last time than a cat had of running from cold water.

And he'd been like a cat, running from water, specifically

bayou water, ever since Mama died and left him and Pop to rattle around the big house in Latanier. Pop was forever arriving from or racing off to an emergency call, and Jeff was left behind to tend to his studies and learn the discipline that would serve him well in his chosen career as a medical researcher.

With the bayou to the south and the country club to the north, he grew into a man with divided loyalties—true to his patrician upbringing yet with a most stubbornly irrepressible urge to return to the murky water his people had called their own for two centuries.

His people.

The thought brought an ungentlemanly snort. Not since he fled the marsh country to study first manners and then medicine had Jeff considered the Acadians *his* people. And yet the documents his father displayed behind glass in his study proclaimed it so. What would his forebears think of him now, years and miles removed from the place they loved?

No matter, he decided. As a doctor of some importance, he would no doubt please them. His own grandfather had been doctor to the bayou people, often spending hours on the water, traveling from birth to death by means of a pirogue, a little canoe given him in lieu of payment. Pop held somewhat to that tradition as well, although his own miles through the bayou were more likely to take place by road rather than the traditional Acadian conveyance.

Jeff, however, was a different man, a doctor without the urge to follow in the tradition of the past two generations. He'd decided early on that there would be no late-night calls to deliver babies or early-morning wake-ups to set broken bones. His was to be the disciplined life of a man bent over a beaker jotting notes that would one day save the world, first in the eradication of influenza and then other diseases. From the happy but disconcerting chaos of his childhood, order would reign.

And reign it had for too many years, but with one trip back to his boyhood home, the reasons for his exile all came tumbling back. Chief among them was a dark-eyed Cajun girl who'd captured his heart, then handed it back to him scarred and broken. Could that be her on the other side of the Nouvelle? Had she changed so little that even at this distance, with the live oaks and the cypress casting her into deep shade, he recognized her?

Jeff removed his hat and swiped at the perspiration on his brow, then cursed himself for a fool. What bayou boy in his right mind would wear his best suit into the marsh? Had he lost that much of his past?

The woman shifted and turned, oblivious to his presence as she knelt at the bank and dipped yet another piece of clothing in the water. With a shrug of her shoulders, she caused her inky hair to ripple and catch the sunlight. Blue-black was the word that came to mind as he stared at the tresses of the beauty in rough clothing.

By the first year away, he'd given no more than a passing glance at the belles of the bayou, preferring instead to keep company with women of the fair-haired variety. Too many memories were dredged up in the familiar, so he sought the unfamiliar.

Thinking on it now, that had to be how he came to leave Louisiana and the bayou forever. *Not forever,* a small voice nagged, *for you're ankle deep in her mud, Old Boy.*

Jeff tore his gaze away from the woman to stare at the mess he'd made of his new wingtips. Why hadn't he planned his wardrobe to fit his activities today? Because the last place he thought he'd end up when he left the house this afternoon was down by the Bayou Nouvelle. He'd hated the Nouvelle, hated its murky depths, hated its dark clusters of trees and the Spanish moss that dipped into her surface like the beards of old men. Most of all he'd hated the memories.

Yet here he stood, inches away from the water and hiding from the woman whose memory had trailed him over the years. A mosquito buzzed his ear, but he knew it was not the ones he heard that could bite. Like thoughts of Angeline Breaux, the real harm was done by the secretive, silent ones.

And yet here you are, the voice nagged. *A real man wouldn't cower in the shadows.*

Jeff shook his head to chase away the mosquito and the thought. Both still lingered just on the edge of his sight.

Angeline Breaux, however, remained in clear view.

How simple it would be to call to her, shouting her name or perhaps a few words of greeting across the black bayou water. What would be the harm in renewing an acquaintance forged years ago?

When she turned his way, Jeff lifted a hand in greeting, then quickly swiped his brow instead. Renewing his friendship with Angeline Breaux would be worse than accepting the mantle of responsibility as bayou doctor from his father.

His was a temporary return, and any contact with the dark-haired beauty might foster a need to stay. As tempting as that might seem, he knew the Lord had another plan for him, a plan that involved much bigger stakes than one displaced man's broken heart.

two

"Angeline!"

Jeff cast about for the origin of the sound and realized it was his own voice. He watched as Angeline jerked her head up, her gaze searching and finally finding his. She mouthed a word, then pressed a hand to her heart, effectively losing the garment she'd been washing in the process.

What had he done? So much for remaining silent and making an easy exit.

"Qui c'est sa? Is that you, Jefferson?"

None but his late grandmother and his most formal professors called him by the appellation. His father had long since banned the use of it, determining that the family forename be cast into history along with its former owners. But from her lips, with the inflection of one born along the banks of the Nouvelle and having never left, the overblown name bore a certain charm.

The garment, a dark mass of what looked to be a pair of man's trousers, inched away, and had he not been struck dumb, Jeff might have mentioned the fact. Instead he merely nodded when she asked, "Jefferson Davis Villare, is that you?"

She stood and dried her hands on her apron. How many times had he lingered at this bank, watching her work at cleaning clothes or some other menial task when he should have been seeing to his studies? Enough so that Pop finally shipped him off to Boston to finish his education properly.

Actually that was only a part of the reason why Pop sent him off. The rest, though unrelated to the bayou itself, had everything to do with Angeline.

It had been years since he stood on this bank and watched

Angeline Breaux, and yet the last time seemed just as fresh and new as if it were merely yesterday. He'd been sent away to learn, and now his education—and the Lord—would take him away permanently. Even so, he stood ankle deep in bayou mud watching Angeline one last time. Funny how things had a way of coming full circle.

"*Bonjour*, Angeline," he finally managed as he inched forward through the muck. "I. . ."

He what? Nothing he cared to admit or speak aloud came to mind, so once again he chose silence. As his gaze dropped to the black water of the bayou, he saw the mass of fabric dislodge and float toward the center of the stream.

Another moment or two and the current would carry it away from Angeline's reach. He really should say something.

"I'm sorry about your papa's passing," she called. "*Sa c'est triste.*"

Jeff redirected his attention to Angeline. "Yes, it was very sad, even though I know he's home with Jesus and Mama. I guess I just expected him to live forever."

An understatement.

Pop had been his rock, the central foundation upon which his life rested. When the busy doctor refused to take to his bed last winter, pneumonia took him to his grave instead. Now Jeff remained behind, the last in a long line of Villares.

She reached to smooth back her hair, and he wondered for a moment why it hadn't been captured into a thick braid as she'd always worn it during their childhood. *Because she's no child, Old Boy.* At least she hadn't succumbed to the hideous fashion of lopping off all but the last bit of length to form it into a bob like the flappers back in Boston.

"So have you come back to stay?" she asked, scattering his thoughts of any place but here.

"No." He answered a bit too quickly and far too loudly. Her startled face confirmed the fact.

"Oh."

Dare he hope she looked the least bit disappointed? "I had to hurry back to school after the funeral. Closing up the house and disposing of a few of Pop's things were postponed until the end of the term."

"I see."

Jeff attempted to venture a few steps forward but felt the warm sludge pull against him.

Affecting a casual stance, he offered Angeline a smile. "Pop never learned how to get rid of anything."

"Oh no. I imagine there must be plenty to go through then."

"You wouldn't believe the bits and pieces I've been finding in his office."

"Really?" The edge of her apron ruffled in the breeze.

"Yes, the medical books will be split between me and Doc Broussard, but there are some things like old pictures and journals that I'm at a loss as to what to do with."

An uncomfortable silence fell between them. "So what brings you this far out of town?" Angeline finally asked.

"You," he almost said, but that wasn't quite right.

No, it wasn't Angeline Breaux herself who drew him to the Bayou Nouvelle but rather the memory of who he used to be when he was with her. Or maybe it was God.

"I suppose the day just seemed right for a sentimental journey," he offered instead.

❧

Sentimental journey?

Angeline shook her head. If only *she* had the time to stand around staring at the water like a fool.

Mais non. With a house full of brothers and sisters to be fed, little Amalie worrying her, and her mama needing the washing done before she could even think of cooking, she had no time to—

The washing!

"Papa's trousers!"

And there they were, heading south toward the Gulf of Mexico just as surely as if she'd put them on a barge and sent them there.

What to do? The day would already end badly if her prayers were answered and Papa arrived without a prospective son-in-law. How much more of his ire would she draw by admitting she'd lost his best trousers while passing the time with Jefferson Villare?

Angeline reached for the stick she used to chase off snakes and leaned out to snag the fabric. To her relief, the end caught on the wet fabric and held tight. Bayou water ran off the legs of Papa's Sunday pants as she lifted them safely out of the current.

Now *she* wouldn't be the reason for his crossness tonight, at least not if she could convince Jefferson to go back to Latanier and leave the bayou to those who belonged there. But just knowing Jefferson Villare had come back to Bayou Nouvelle would be enough to keep Papa rattling the rafters of their little cabin with his complaints long after her poor tired mama and the babies had gone to bed.

A glance in Jefferson's direction drew a sigh along with a touch of embarrassment at her lapse in attention. *Where had the years gone?*

"Angeline? *Quoi y a?*"

"The matter?" She shrugged. *"Pas rien."*

Not the complete truth, of course, telling him nothing was wrong. Oh, but she did like hearing the Acadian words and the way the old Jefferson Villare came through in them.

When he spoke to her in the language of their childhood, the Acadian of their parents, grandparents, and others too old to remember, she could almost close her eyes and believe nothing had changed between them. That the years had not rolled by like the black water of the Nouvelle.

That he hadn't gone far beyond Bayou Nouvelle—and her.

"T'es sur de sa, Ma Chere?"

Ma Chere? He hadn't called her by that pet name in how many years? "Yes," she said quickly. "I'm sure."

Again, she'd been less than fully truthful in her answer. *Mais non, just look at him, the city boy in his fine clothes. So handsome, so—*

Angeline recognized the source of the loud snap before she felt the stick break.

"Arête!" But the contrary trousers did not stop. Rather they headed downstream as if they knew she would give chase.

And so she did.

At first she loped along on foot, dodging beneath the low limb and sweeping skirt of a weeping willow and hurdling a palmetto as she kept pace with the trousers. Seizing a fallen sweet gum branch nearly as thick as Papa's arm, she raced ahead of her prize and waded into the water ankle deep, gathering the hem of her skirt with her free hand to keep it dry. Leaning out as far as she could, she just brushed the tip of the branch beneath the floating trousers.

"Gete toi, Angeline!"

"I am watching out for myself," she snapped.

As if the city boy had never seen her ankle deep in the bayou. Why, many a day the both of them had shucked their work—her, the washing or some other job Mama had assigned, and he, the schooling his papa felt to be so important—

"Angeline, come out of the water and let them go. *Sa vaut pas la peine.*"

"Yes, they *are* worth it, and Papa will have my hide if I lose them." She looked up to see Jefferson pushing through a stand of reed and cattails to frown at her. "How many times did you laugh at me when I dropped something or another in the water and had to fetch it?"

His worried look eased and a grin began to dawn. "And

how many times did you dare me to throw it so the both of us could go swimming?"

Somehow his grin irritated her. Maybe it was because he stood dry on the bank and she alone was left standing in the Bayou Nouvelle.

No, those things were just the here and now. It was the past that irked her—what could have happened and what did.

"We were silly children, but now the games are done and so are we."

A fast-moving current caught one leg of the trousers and dragged the entire soggy mess—and her—toward the middle of the bayou, hauling her under.

three

Angeline emerged sputtering and wiped the muddy water from her eyes. When she spied the trousers drifting toward the opposite bank, she dove after them only to be jerked backward.

"Let me go!" She pummeled blindly at the thing holding her and fought to gain her footing. "I mean it!"

If a gator had her, she would go down fighting. If it were something else, like a rabid dog or a wild boar or maybe even one of those big brown bears Ernest and Papa sometimes shot, she stood a good chance of getting away if she could just keep moving. If it was one of her brothers pulling a prank, the more blows she landed the better.

"Arête. Be still!" It was Jefferson, his voice near enough to be. . .

Whirling around, she came eye-to-eye with him. Soaked to the skin from his chest down, he bore a nasty scratch across his left cheek, no doubt from her hand. His fancy summer suit was streaked with mud, and his bowler hat floated past as if it were giving chase to Papa's trousers.

"I have to get those pants. Just let me be." She wrenched out of his grip and started after the trousers only to have the stubborn man restrain her once more. "Are you crazy?" she shouted.

"Are you?" His voice was soft, deadly calm, and he barely moved except to gather her close to him. *"Tas toi,"* he whispered.

First he manhandled her and then demanded she stop talking? How dare he? And the way he held her, well, if she thought on it, it made her blush for sure.

As she watched little streams of bayou water trace a path

down the side of Jefferson's neck, Angeline tried not to think of what it might look like should someone come along and catch them like this. She might be an uneducated girl and an old maid at that, but she knew improper when she saw it. Anyone passing by would think the same thing for sure.

Again.

She pressed both palms against his chest and pushed hard. He didn't budge.

"Let me go," she said, panic beginning to rise. *"S'il vous plaît."* What if he meant to take by force what she'd shamefully wanted to offer all those years ago?

Her heart began to pound, and she cast a glance at the sun to see where it stood in the sky. If only she could remember how long she'd been at her work.

Surely Mama would send her sister Mathilde or brothers Julien or Martin to fetch her for lunch soon. Maybe Amalie would wander back. But what could they do?

Julien was as fast as Tante Flo's rooster and Martin could swim like a duck, but neither boy could best a man of Jefferson's size. And Mathilde, well, with her mind full of the silliness of a girl who wants to be a woman, she paid more attention to her reflection in the bayou than anything else.

Like as not, she'd miss the scene entirely if she caught sight of a honeysuckle vine that could be woven into her braid. Only little Amalie, the nine year old, would have the sense to do something, anything, to rescue her sister. But Amalie had probably fallen asleep even though she complained that she wouldn't.

No, she was on her own.

Angeline tried one last desperate move—reasoning with the fool. *"J'sus parti a la maison,"* she said.

"Non." His grip tightened. "You can't go home yet, *Ma Chere*. Look behind you." Little by little, he raised his free hand to point to the opposite bank, where a mama gator

watched them closely while her two little ones lay sunning themselves at her side.

Angeline froze. She had seen some big gators in her time, but this one was huge. And, judging from the way it followed their every move while edging its toothy snout toward the water, the beast was hungry as well.

"She's not going to get us, understand?"

Their gazes met and Angeline nodded. "Yes."

"Okay, I plan to walk out of this bayou with all my arms and legs, and you're going with me, so hold on tight and don't say a word."

"But, I—"

"Hush." He hitched her nearer and she stifled a gasp. "You might want to start praying now, *Ma Chere*. That old alligator, she's looking at me like she's in love."

Angeline buried her head against his shoulder and did as he said, silently begging *Le Bon Dieu* to get them out of this mess. Jefferson began taking slow, easy steps backward.

When she heard the loud splash that signaled the gator had tired of waiting, Angeline scrambled out of Jefferson's arms and dove toward the bank. No matter how fast that old gator could swim, she prayed Papa had taught her to swim faster.

But instead of swimming, she felt herself rise from the water, caught up in Jefferson's arms. "What are you doing?"

"No time to explain. Just hold tight."

He raced with her onto the bank and thrust her toward the bent branch of a cypress tree. Scrambling up just ahead of the gator, Jefferson fought for his grip on the branch with wet hands.

"Hurry, Jefferson! It's right behind you."

He made a swipe at the limb and missed. "Back up," he said as he reached for it again. "I'm afraid I'll pull you down."

"I'm stronger than I look."

Angeline caught hold of his wrist and held tight to the

tree's gnarled trunk as she helped haul him up just seconds before the gator's claws hit the wood. A moment later, Jefferson perched beside her, his breath coming in ragged gasps, while the alligator made noisy circles beneath them.

"That was close," he said.

"*Oui,*" she whispered. "Too close."

&

Too close indeed, both the encounter with the alligator and with this woman.

Jeff expelled a long breath and waited for his racing heart to slow. He cast a glance at his companion, flushed a pretty pink and still as wide-eyed as she'd been moments ago in the bayou. Funny, the alligator's menace paled in comparison to the trouble he could find up here in the tree.

As long as he'd known her, Jeff had never thought of Angeline Breaux as a delicate creature, but now she looked as fragile as his mother's favorite china teacup. He knew he'd have to watch her carefully for any signs of shock.

As a man you've been doing that ever since you caught sight of her, Old Boy.

He shook his head and cleared the thought. "*T'es puer?*"

Jeff cringed and looked away. *Of course she's afraid, you idiot.* A check below proved the alligator had neither left nor slowed her pacing. *Think of something intelligent to say, something to take her mind off her fear.* "Remember when I dared you to kiss a frog and your papa caught you and thought you'd lost your good sense?"

They'd been fearless back then, the two of them. Only the Lord and their parents held their behavior in check. Sometimes he thought of those times, reminded of the simple innocence by the flicker of a firefly or the chirp of a cricket.

Her shoulders sagged an inch. "You told me a handsome prince would come and take me away if I did, and I figured if I had to kiss a frog to get out of the bayou, I'd do it."

The tiniest of smiles dawned, and she cast her gaze in his direction. He had caused that smile. His chest swelled despite the gravity of the situation. "That's better."

Angeline looked away. The smile faded. "You're bleeding and your suit is ruined."

Jeff swiped at his face and felt dried blood crumble beneath his fingers. At some point he'd have to treat it, but for now it seemed to be nothing more than a minor inconvenience. His suit, however, was another story entirely. He'd have to arrange for Pop's tailor to make another before he left for New York. This one was a total loss.

Another glance at Angeline told him her frock had fared no better. The white apron had muddied to a dull brown where the current had dragged her across the bayou floor, and her dress. . .well, he preferred not to look too close at the damp and clinging frock.

When he slipped out of his jacket and placed it around her shoulders, her color deepened but she did not protest. Rather she gathered the soggy material around her and began to fret with the brass button on the right sleeve.

Beneath them the alligator seemed to be losing interest. Jeff leaned against the tree's knotty trunk and stared through the branches at the clear Louisiana sky. Under other circumstances, a man could have spent a considerable amount of time in this spot and called it relaxation.

"Jefferson?"

He cut her a sideways glance. "Yes."

"You could've stayed close and gone to the medical college at Baton Rouge, you know."

"I know."

"Why'd you up and leave? The real reason, I mean, and not what your papa told everyone about Boston being the 'best place to further your education.' " Her pensive voice caught him off guard while her dead-on imitation of Pop made him chuckle.

Why indeed? Half a dozen plausible explanations came to mind. None were the real reason.

"I suppose it had something to do with you." There, he'd finally said it.

Their gazes locked. Her thick hair had begun to dry in soft tendrils, framing a face that could hold its own against any of the heavily painted and powdered flappers back in Boston.

A face that most likely attracted many a suitor among the boys of the bayou.

four

He swallowed a gulp and asked the question to which he had no right to know the answer. "Is there someone special, *Ma Chere?*" He paused and cleared his throat before he could continue. "Or maybe you have a husband and three or four *bebes?*"

"*Non,*" she said quickly. Was that shame that crossed her pretty features? "I never found someone who could believe I was. . ." She paused. "That is, everyone thought we had, well. . ."

His heart wrenched. He knew what everyone thought. When Pop put him on the first train north, it was all too obvious he thought the same thing.

If only something *had* happened between them. No, that was wrong, he quickly amended.

Both he and Angeline had honored the Lord and waited on Him to lead the direction of their relationship. He'd always wondered why God hadn't honored them in return, why he'd been allowed to rise above the whispered talk while Angeline was forced to stay behind and endure it.

Another unsettling thought to discard; another reason to flee the bayou and the past.

"My life is good, Jefferson," Angeline said without warning. Why didn't he believe her?

"With another one on the way, Mama needs me more than ever. And my little brothers and sisters, they're like my own babies, all of them. Well, except for Mathilde, but she's so silly. *Elle est amorouse.*"

"Little Mathilde, boy crazy?" He shook his head. "I don't believe it."

"She's plenty old enough. Older by nearly a year than I was

when you left and ready to be married off when it's her turn."
The statement hung heavy between them.

"It seems like yesterday, us spending time together."

Angeline nodded with a wry smile. "But I don't recall us ever spending much time in a tree."

"Mais non," he said.

"So, what is it you're going to do with yourself now that you've finished medical school and graduated with honors?"

"How did you know that?"

She upped her smile a notch. "The bayou, it's a small place, Jefferson. Everyone knows everything about everyone."

"Ah," he said with a nod. "I suppose I'd forgotten." He studied the face of his friend, then cleared his throat. "Actually, I'm going to be doing medical research."

"So you're not going to be a doctor?"

"Yes, I'll still be considered a doctor, but I won't be treating patients." When she looked confused, he felt the need to explain. "You see, I've been given an opportunity to do research and I'm very excited about it."

"Oh?"

Jeff nodded. "Yes, I'll be working at Columbia University's College of Physicians and Surgeons in New York. I was asked to join a team of doctors who are researching a cure for influenza and the complications of pneumonia. It's very exciting."

Her expression told him it was more confusing to her than exciting. "That's nice," she said.

Once again silence fell between them. Generally Jeff found it easy to talk to the fairer sex. Where were his wit and charm now? Most likely drowned in the black water of the bayou.

"Well, now, it looks like our friend's gone." Jeff gestured toward the opposite bank, where a mother and child reunion was taking place among the alligators. "What say we take our leave, *Mademoiselle?*"

He scrambled down and turned to help Angeline to the ground. A glance over his shoulder told him the creatures had lost interest in the taste of humans, at least for the moment. When the last one disappeared into the undergrowth, he relaxed.

"Allons, Angeline. I'll walk with you."

She looked as if she might argue, but then she nodded. He fell in step beside her, and they walked along the path that snaked by the bayou in companionable silence.

Jefferson committed each detail to memory—the warm sun on his back as his wet shirt stuck to his damp skin, the call of the mockingbird as it fled the diminutive dogwood tree, and most of all the dark-haired woman as she strolled barefoot and beautiful beside him.

"So up in New York, what will you do with yourself?" Angeline asked.

Jeff shrugged and affected a jaunty stance, pretending to tip the hat he no longer wore. "Medical research is exciting enough and I don't have any other plans. That's what God has called me to do. And you, what's in your future?"

She seemed to consider the statement, all the while looking past him at the bayou. *"Sa fait pas rien."*

He stopped short and grasped her by the shoulders. "It *does* matter, Angeline. Never say it doesn't." She tried to duck out of his grasp, but he wouldn't allow it. "Are you going to let wagging tongues and gossip keep you down? People *talk some,* but God alone *knows all."*

Jeff felt her shoulders tense beneath his fingers. When her gaze collided with his, he felt the jolt deep in his gut. He scrambled to think of something, anything, to fill the desperate silence. *Help me know what to say, God.*

"You used to have such dreams." The words tumbled out, and he prayed they were from the Lord and not from his scrambled brain. "What happened?"

"That's all they were, Jefferson, dreams." She spat the words at him as if he were the cause.

"Dreams can come true," he said. "Women are doing all sorts of things now. Why, just last week in New York I saw a woman who—"

"You have no idea what you're talking about. Look at you." She cast a disdainful glance at him. "You're the great and perfect Dr. Jefferson Villare. You've never had to do anything in your life that you didn't want to. Nobody's ever told you what to think or who to be."

Jeff opened his mouth to argue but thought better of it. "Okay," he said slowly, "what's the one thing you always wanted to do but never did?"

Her eyes narrowed. Good, he'd struck a chord. Maybe with a little more encouragement, this shrinking violet just might bloom yet.

She tilted her chin and gave him a sideways look. "You really want to know?"

The challenge surprised and delighted him. *This* was the Angeline he remembered. "Why, yes, in fact I dare you to—"

Her kiss, laid just an inch off center of his lips, stopped him from finishing the provocation. Too soon, she took a step backward and covered her mouth with trembling fingers.

"I'm sorry, *excusez moi.* I don't know what I was thinking." With that she bolted and ran, darting so close to Bayou Nouvelle that several times Jeff felt sure he'd be carrying her out of it again.

When he caught her, he planned to tell her there was no need for apologies among old friends; that a kiss shared in secret would remain a secret. Instead, he reached her just yards from where he'd first seen her and, without comment, wrapped her in his arms, still damp and smelling of bayou water.

"You missed," he whispered as he showed her exactly how two sets of lips should match up.

The kiss might have continued indefinitely had the click of a shotgun against Jeff's ear not brought the proceedings to a screeching halt.

"Take your hands off my baby girl, Villare, and I *might* be convinced to let you leave this stretch o' bayou by some way other'n the undertaker."

Jeff froze and cut his gaze toward the sound. Theophile Breaux stood inches away, his angry countenance eclipsed only by the matching look of ire on his eldest son Ernest's face. Behind them a stranger stood taking in the scene with a blank expression.

Jeff could only pray this man was the new pastor at the local church or perhaps an itinerant preacher set on a nice meal and an afternoon nap beneath the overhang of the Breauxs' front porch. Given the temperament of Villare men, the stranger could be his only hope of escape.

Angeline slipped out of Jeff's grasp, and had Ernest not enveloped her in a bear hug, she might have reached the path to her cabin in short order. Instead she stood motionless. The stranger shifted to stare at Angeline, his expression still unreadable.

"Pleased to see you again, Monsieur Breaux." Jeff forced the apprehension from his voice and attempted a pleasantry in the older man's native tongue. *"Comment ca va?"*

"Ain't no bidness o' yours how I is," he said, "but rather you ought to ask how steady a hand I've got these days."

To his credit, Theophile seemed not to have the slightest tremor. The barrel of the shotgun still rested against Jeff's temple, the only shaking possibly his own.

Now what, Lord?

"Doc Broussard tole me you been closin' up that big house o' your papa's over t' Latanier an gettin' rid o' his things," Theophile said.

Jeff swallowed hard and gave thanks for what looked like the beginning of a civil conversation. "Yes, Sir, that's right. I have."

He could stand here all day facing the old man, but Angeline shouldn't have to endure the humiliation. The fault for the situation was his alone.

"Then if you gots bidness in Latanier, I don't reckon you got any bidness down here." He peered down the barrel, then shook his head. The strangest look of sadness passed over his tanned, weathered features. *"Sa fini pas."*

It never ends? What an odd thing to say.

"Il n'a in bon boute, Villare," Ernest said flatly.

Jeff smiled. "Yes, it has been a good while, Ernest," he managed to say without taking his gaze off the gun. Perhaps his former fishing buddy had finally come to his senses. "How about letting Angeline go, old friend?"

No response. His hopes for rescue plummeted.

"She had nothing to do with this. You see, she was just minding her own business when I—"

"When you mistook her for her sister Mathilde and let your heart run off wid your good sense." Theophile lowered the shotgun and stared at Jeff, then cocked his head to one side. "Now ain't that right?"

Had the Acadian lost his mind along with his good sense? He'd never even been on speaking terms with little Mathilde, much less anything resembling what he suggested. "Well, Sir, I really don't know what you—"

"Theophile Breaux, what on earth have you gone and done? Put that shotgun away afore someone gets hurt, eh?"

An obviously pregnant Clothilde Breaux pushed past her husband to clasp Jeff's hand into hers. The years had been kind to the woman, and he could see much of her eldest daughter in her graceful bearing and unassuming beauty.

"Good morning, Mrs. Breaux."

"Jefferson Villare, is that you?"

When he nodded and said, "Yes, Ma'am," she released his

hand to drag him into a tight embrace.

A moment later she held him at arm's length and gave him an appraising look. "You're a sight for sore eyes, for sure, you. Look at you all growed up and handsome and. . ." She paused and then touched his cheek. "What happened to you?"

"Actually I—"

"Theophile, what you gone an' done to this boy here?" She turned her attention to her husband, hands on her hips. "He look like he done been dropped by his feets into the shallow end of the bayou, then rolled over by a big ole gator. Is this how we treat Doc Villare's boy? After his papa done come doctor you for nothin' but a pot o' Angeline's gumbo an' a couple a eggs from my layin' hen? Be ashamed."

Before Theophile could protest, Clothilde pried the shotgun from his fingers and handed the weapon to Angeline. "Scoot on up to the house with this an' put it somewhere safe, eh, *Bebe?* You an' me, we talk about this later when the mens aren't underfoot."

When Angeline hesitated, her mother turned to Jeff. "Walk her home, would you, eh? She don't look like she could find a piece a straw in a hay bale about now." She leaned in close and winked. "I can handle her papa, but you'd best skedaddle quick till I do."

Jeff nodded. *"Oui, Madame Breaux, merci beaucoup."*

"You don't got to thank me, no. You papa, he a good man, and you dear mama, a real lady if I never did saw none, Lord rest they souls. They raise you right, to go to church an' love the Lord, an' that's what a good mama and papa do, eh?"

"Yes, Ma'am," he said.

"That's right. Now you know you welcome here always, eh? Say, how 'bout you come back for supper?"

Possibly the worst idea he'd heard since deciding to take a quick side trip to the bayou this morning. And yet it held a certain appeal.

"I couldn't really."

But as he said the words, he caught Angeline's gaze and felt his resolve weaken. A few more hours with her before he took his leave permanently did sound enticing, even if it meant enduring her overprotective father and strangely menacing brother.

Clothilde nudged him and smiled. "Angeline's gone make us up a mess o' shrimps and gumbo. You still like that, don't you?"

"Yes, Ma'am."

In truth he hadn't had shrimp gumbo since he left for Boston. Even during holidays back at home, he hadn't been able to bring himself to partake. No one could make gumbo like Angeline Breaux anyway, so why bother?

"Just like you daddy a lovin' that gumbo. Well, *je va vous voir plus tard*, Young Man," Clothilde said loudly to Jeff before placing his hand on Angeline's elbow and giving them both a shove. "Now scoot, the both of you."

"You won't be seeing him later, an' that's fo' sure, Clothilde Breaux," he heard Theophile say. "And take yo' hand off my girl, Villare, or you'll draw back a nub next time you try it."

"Yes, Sir," he said as he quickly complied.

"Hush now, Theophile. Have you left your manners back in town, eh?" Clothilde asked. "We might be poor folk, but the good Lord still expects us to be charitable. The Villare boy's coming back for supper and that's that. Now who is this nice young man you've brought to see us today?"

five

Angeline shouldered Papa's shotgun and lit out down the path toward home. What had she done? Losing Papa's Sunday trousers was nothing compared to what just happened. In front of God, her papa and brother, and who knows who else, she'd kissed Jefferson Breaux like the Jezebel they all thought she was.

She allowed an ironic chuckle as she tried in vain to balance the big gun and keep Jefferson's jacket hanging around her shoulders. At least she hadn't disappointed them.

If only the kiss hadn't been all she'd imagined—and more.

No, she couldn't think on it any further. Papa brought a man home from town and, unless she missed her guess, the man was for her. Now she had to go home, get herself cleaned up, and cook a meal. To make it worse, Jefferson tagged a half step behind her.

There would be no rest for the weary—or the humiliated—today.

Angeline whirled around and put out a hand to stop her shadow. He pulled up just short of running her over. "Stop following me."

"Just following orders. I told your mother I would see you got home, and she isn't someone I'd like to cross." He shrugged and gave her that goofy smile she used to find so cute. "Besides, you've got my jacket."

Sliding the damp coat off her shoulders, she thrust it toward him. "Here, now go home," she stated as calmly as she could. "I can find my way back just fine."

"I'm sure you can, *Ma Chere*," he said as he folded the

jacket over his left arm and linked his right arm with hers. "Still, I'm going to keep my word and walk you home."

It was the fastest walk Angeline ever took. By the time she'd wrenched free of Jefferson's grip and crossed the porch to close the door behind her, she was out of breath. Her apron hung limp and her skirt stuck to the backs of her legs as she leaned, eyes closed, against the heavy old cypress door.

"Lord, what am I going to do?" she whispered.

"You're going to move out of the way and let Papa and that handsome man in, Angie."

Angeline opened her eyes to see Mathilde standing at the hearth, baby Eileen on her hip and the four-year-old twins on the floor at her feet. Amalie hid behind her skirts, still looking flushed.

Before Angeline could say something back, Papa's heavy footsteps rocked the wood beneath her feet. She stepped out of the way just before the big door crashed open and Papa filled the doorway.

Eileen began to wail, and Mama slipped past Papa to grab the baby and bundle her outside. The boys toddled behind her, oblivious to the situation. When Mama called Mathilde and Amalie to follow them, Angeline found herself alone in the cabin with Papa and the stranger.

What Mathilde called handsome Angeline preferred to call merely pleasant, at least in comparison to the city boy who'd just left. He had a kind face, this man who looked to be only a few years older than she, and a mouth that appeared capable of a broad smile. Now, however, he held his lips in a tight line, and only the slight tint of red on his cheeks hinted to Angeline that embarrassment might be the cause of his own discomfort.

For an eternity, Papa stood staring at her, taking in every inch of her wet and muddy clothing, her damp hair, and her shame. Hot tears threatened, but somehow she managed to hold them back. Outside of disappointing her heavenly Father, disappointing her earthly one was possibly the worst thing she could ever think to do.

She'd only done it once before, and the pain of that moment still stung.

"Nicolas Arceneaux," Papa finally said, "meet my eldest daughter, Angeline."

Mr. Arceneaux gave Papa a quick nod, then wiped his palm against the bib of his overalls before thrusting his hand toward Angeline. He mumbled a few words of greeting, eyes averted, and she responded as she'd been taught.

"May I offer you coffee, Monsieur Arceneaux?" she added when a sideways glance caught sight of Papa's frown.

"Fetch the pot quick, Girl," Papa said. "We've business to discuss, eh, Arceneaux?"

The look that passed between them told Angeline they had already been in discussion. Unfortunately, it didn't take a city education to know what they'd talked about. As she headed for the summer kitchen, she cast a glance over her shoulder at the man who could someday be her husband and sighed.

"So what you think of my girl?" she heard Papa ask. "She all I tole you an' more, eh?"

"She is indeed, although. . . ," she heard Arceneaux say before Papa's laughter and the closing of the front door drowned out the rest of his statement.

As she passed by the open window, she slowed her steps to listen again. This time Papa's words were clear. "The man, he is nothing to her. *T'es trompe.*"

But *was* he mistaken? Angeline carried that question all the way to the summer kitchen and back onto the porch. As she set the coffee in front of the men, she looked into the eyes of Nicolas Arceneaux and heard the answer.

He is mistaken. The man—Jefferson Davis Villare—is indeed something to me.

But what? And even if she could figure it out, what could she do? How could she stop this thing Papa had already set into motion?

"She's just shy, that's all," she heard Papa say a moment before he jerked the coffeepot from her hand. "You pour yourself some o' my Mathilde's good coffee, an' me and Angeline, we be right back, eh?"

Papa's hand clamped around Angeline's wrist and jerked her toward the door. Out in the yard, he brought her to an abrupt stop beside his tool shed.

"What you think you doin', baby girl?" he demanded. "That man there, he a good man what wants to make you his wife, an' you go an' throw youself on some boy what run off an' don't even give you the time of day for all these years?"

"I'm sorry, Papa."

He released her and stood back to look at her as if he were seeing her for the first time. A second later, his harsh features softened.

"My girl, she's good, an' I know it." He swept his hand toward the bayou. "But people 'round here, they don't know what I know, eh? Not a one o' them gone let they boys come 'round here after you long as they think you. . ."

Papa's words faded and he cast a glance skyward. Angeline bit her lip as the first tear fell.

"To find you a husband, you gone have to go somewhere else, but I don't want nobody to take you off o' this bayou," he continued, his voice rough. "Angeline, this man, he promised me he'll not take you away. He got a boat an' he fishes down t' the Gulf. He need a good woman what to help him and to give him strong sons." Papa reached to take Angeline into his arms. *"Le Bon Dieu,* He tole me this morning you was gone meet your husband today, baby girl."

Angeline buried her face in the familiar curve of Papa's shoulder. "He did?"

"Oui," he whispered as he smoothed her hair, then held her out at arm's length. "Now get yourself cleaned up an' set to cookin' the gumbo, eh?"

Angeline swiped at a tear and chose her words carefully. "Papa," she said slowly, "when God told you I would meet my husband today, did He specifically say it would be Mr. Arceneaux?"

Papa's eyes narrowed and his face flushed bright red. "Get on in that house an' do as you're tole, Angeline Breaux. I ain't gone talk about this no more."

❧

Easing into the welcoming softness of Pop's favorite chair, Jeff leaned his head against the smooth leather and tried to make sense of the morning. With all he could want in the way of things to think about and deal with spread across Pop's desk, his mind couldn't settle on any of them. Instead, his focus kept returning to Angeline Breaux.

"Busy?"

Jeff looked up to see Doc Broussard leaning against the doorframe, his ancient black medical bag caught in the crook of his arm. When Jeff smiled and stood, his father's dearest friend approached to envelope Jeff in a bear hug.

"You know I'm never too busy to see you, Sir," Jeff said.

To his credit, the man said nothing of Jeff's rumpled appearance and the still untreated scratch on his cheek. Instead, he dropped the well-worn satchel, settled into the chair across from Jeff, and perused the thick stacks of papers littering its surface. "Made any headway in all this?"

"Does it look like it?"

Doc studied him a moment. "Actually, it looks like you've been busy with something altogether different. Dare an old man to ask what that might be?"

"You could ask."

"But you're not going to tell me." He smiled. "I understand.

It's just my meddling ways, you know. After all, either your papa or I delivered just about every baby born in this parish in the last thirty years—you and Miss Angeline Breaux included." He paused and feigned innocence. "Not that I'm of a mind to think you've been down to Bayou Nouvelle today."

"You heard?"

Doc's smile bloomed into a full-fledged chuckle. "Gertie Cousins had it on good authority from Teensie Landry, who heard it from Enola Joseph, that your daddy's Model A was left beside the road a skip and a jump from the Bayou Nouvelle. I believe it was Marie Boudreaux who added that it was just a quarter mile or so upriver from the Breaux property, although Ouida Simon said she thought it was more like a half mile."

Jeff leaned back again and contemplated what the wagging tongues of the parish would make of it if they knew any more details of his morning. Absently, he touched his cheek. He thanked the Lord that no one had seen his dip in the bayou or watched Angeline's endearing attempt at a kiss.

Or his more practiced response.

"Better let me take a look at that scratch," Doc said. "You got to be careful with bayou water this time of year." Again, the old man feigned innocence while he made a fuss of examining Jeff's wound. "Looks like it just needs a bit of cleaning." The doctor reached into his bag. "Let me just see what I've got in here." He made quite a show of fishing around in the battered satchel. "Ah, here it is." Instead of cleaning solution, Doc Broussard produced a pair of dark trousers.

Theophile Breaux's trousers. Jeff wanted to crawl under the desk.

"The reverend recognized them right off," Doc said.

"What does Reverend Dautrive have to do with this?"

"Well, you see, Theophile never misses a Sunday service, and he and the family sit right down in front, just a few feet from the pulpit." Doc looked at him like his answer made perfect sense, then thrust the damp trousers toward Jeff. "If you've got any plans to go out there before you leave, you might want to bring these along. Theophile probably won't miss them until Sunday morning."

"*If* I have plans?" Jeff gave him a sideways look, then balled up the trousers, tossing them into the corner. "Your sources didn't tell you I'm invited for gumbo tonight?"

All innocence once more, Doc shook his head and rose. "My sources? I don't know what you're talking about, and I don't have the time to sit and figure it out. I'm afraid we're going to have another nasty outbreak of influenza."

"Let's hope it doesn't spread like last time," Jeff said. *Like when it took my mother,* he left unsaid. "Let me know if you need help seeing patients. I'll do what I can while I'm here."

"I appreciate that, Jeff, but I pray it won't be necessary." He paused. "However, the invitation is always open to join me in my practice. I could sorely use the help."

"No," sprang from Jeff's lips much too quickly. "As much as I would love it, I'm afraid God has called me elsewhere."

"Well, I never make it a practice to argue with the good Lord." The old doctor regarded him. "You sure you can handle all this?"

"All what?"

"Everything. I don't know how you're going to get it all sorted through before Wednesday." He gestured toward the desk. "You got any idea what you're going to do with all that? Beyond the books and medical papers, I mean."

Jeff shrugged. "I'm still deciding. As for the house, I think it's time to sell."

"I see." If he had an opinion, his expression did not give it away. "Well, I understand there's a fortune to be made in stocks these days. Maybe you ought to go that route first before you start thinking of selling your family home. There are a whole lot of happy memories in this old place."

Jeff tapped his temple. "There are a lot of happy memories up here too, Sir."

"Yes, well, I see your point." Doc scooped up his satchel and headed for the door, stopping as he reached the threshold. "I do have it on good authority that Angeline Breaux's shrimp gumbo is the best in south Louisiana. I took a pot of Miss Angeline's gumbo in payment for delivering Clothilde's last three babies, you know. Don't know if I'll last until the fall, when the next one's set to arrive. Maybe you could ask for an extra bowl for me."

"Very funny, Doc," Jeff called as he hurried to walk his guest to the door. "Say, you seem to know a lot. I don't suppose any of the folks you talked to today mentioned the name of the fellow Theophile Breaux brought home today."

The old man stopped short and turned to face Jeff. For a moment he looked as if he might answer, but after a few seconds he shook his head and walked away. "I believe you'll find that out soon enough," he called.

Jeff watched Doc Broussard shuffle down the steps and disappear around the corner. His age really had begun to show. How long before the work hours wore him down like Pop? He shook off the thought along with the nagging idea of taking Doc's employment offer to the Lord for His opinion.

"You still here, Mr. Jeff?" his father's housekeeper, the formidable matron known as Mrs. Mike, called from the kitchen.

He followed the voice to the kitchen, where Mrs. Mike had just placed two steaming peach pies on the sideboard. "Yes, Ma'am, I'm here," he said as he stopped short. "Why did you cook two pies?"

She mopped her brow with the corner of her apron and drew herself up to her full height. "I ain't gone send you out t' sit down at Clothilde Breaux's table without you carrying a pie t' go wit the gumbo. It wouldn't be polite, and your dear departed mama and papa would have my hide when I see them up in heaven."

Jeff shook his head. "You knew I was going out there tonight." He paused. "But Doc just left, so he couldn't have told you and I don't think I mentioned it."

"What that got to do wit anything, Mr. Jeff?" she said as she folded her apron back into place. "Can't an old woman bake a pie or two without all these questions?"

Jeff leaned against the cabinet. "How long does it take you to make a good pie, Mrs. Mike?"

"Well, let me see. Once I get me the peaches cut just right I. . ." Her eyes narrowed. "Now don't you try to start with me, Mr. Jeff. You might be all growed up and a doctor like your daddy, but you always gonna be a young 'un to me, you understand?"

"Yes, Ma'am," Jeff said with a chuckle. "Say, I'll be needing a suit of clothes ironed before this evening. Do you mind?"

"I already done that," she said, "but if you'll fetch me Mr. Breaux's pants, I'll have them looking just as nice as new afore it's time for you t' go."

"How'd you know about. . ." He paused. "Oh, never mind."

six

The gumbo was terrible. Angeline knew it without being told. She'd put too much of something, or maybe not enough.

Whatever the problem, the only fix for it was to toss out the whole pot and start over again. She hoisted the pot and turned to throw it to the dogs, only to run into her mother. The gumbo sloshed and threatened to spill, but she leveled the pot in time to whirl it back around onto the stove.

Looking down, she realized she'd saved the very gumbo she meant to throw out while she'd ruined her one good dress in the process. At least she hadn't been burned by the hot roux.

"Goodness, *Bebe*, you don't have to carry that heavy thing. Let the mens come on out an get it." Before she could respond, her mother shoved her toward the house. "Now you go on and get yourself prettied up afore someone sees you wearin' the gumbo, eh?"

A few minutes later, Angeline stood among the wreckage of two ruined dresses. One still brown and streaked with mud from the bayou and the other wearing gumbo roux in splotches across the front.

The only dress left in the armoire was her Sunday dress, and she could hardly show herself downstairs in that on a Friday evening. Why, it would look like she was headed for church instead of. . .

Her mind caught on the thought of Sunday clothes and hung there. Papa's trousers.

"Oh no!"

❧

Jeff circled the path twice before setting his feet toward the

Breaux cabin, the peach pie in a tin tucked into the crook of his arm and the trousers wrapped in brown paper and tied with a string. Leave it to Mrs. Mike to think of a way to return Mr. Breaux's trousers without making a fuss. Now if he could just hand off the package to Angeline without drawing attention to the fact.

Surely the Lord would do the both of them this small favor. Neither he nor Angeline needed to face any more ire from Theophile Breaux.

Deep threads of purple and orange decorated the edges of the sky and danced across the waves on the bayou. Beneath Jeff's feet, the hard-packed terrain wore a layer of decaying leaves, each step sending up the earthy scent so peculiar to south Louisiana to tease his nose.

And the sounds—no words could do justice to the symphony of bayou creatures when they began their evening songs. It was the music of his childhood, the anthem of his youth. Soon it would be the sound of a fading memory.

Wednesday morning he would climb aboard a train headed north and trade those brilliant hues and fresh scents for a city where progress made up for beauty and symphonies were conducted only within the hallowed halls of the opera house.

And Wednesday would be here ever so soon.

What had he been thinking? An evening of stolen happiness—a lifetime of what-ifs—that's what Jeff would face if he continued with his ridiculous notion to actually sit at a table with Angeline Breaux and her father.

He squared his shoulders and picked up his pace. It would be neither, he determined. Tonight would merely serve as a good-bye to the bayou and the life he must sacrifice to do what God created him to do.

Tomorrow was Saturday, a good day to finish collecting the things he wanted sent to his apartment in New York. Sunday would be a day of worship, of course, and Monday would bring more decisions. He would call on Pop's lawyer that day to start the process of selling the big old place. Tuesday would be reserved for packing and last-minute errands, and Wednesday morning he would be on the train to New York. By Friday his well-ordered life would resume, and he would probably find himself working the weekend in the lab just to catch up with his research.

He cradled the pie and stepped over a protruding root, nearly losing his balance, the package, and the pie in the process. Yes, he decided as he righted himself, it would be good to get back to his comfortable routine—to his quiet life.

He heard the noise before he actually saw the cabin. A chorus of sounds, male and female, echoed among the trees and seemed to shake the tails of the Spanish moss. A lone fiddle played soft and low, a mere accompaniment to the true Acadian concerto—the Acadians themselves.

Rounding the corner, he stepped into the clearing. With the sun behind the wood frame home, the front yard lay bathed partially in shadow. In places across the lawn, if one could call the expanse of green and brown a lawn, groups of men and boys stood in clusters while children ran among them.

Jeff searched the crowd for a glimpse of Angeline. He even stared hard into the lighted windows to capture a glance of her. Finally his gaze landed on the porch and a group of older women.

Clothilde Breaux stepped away from a knot of ladies on the porch to meet him halfway. "Well, there you are, Jefferson Villare. Come on over here."

After a mind-numbing introduction to aunts, cousins, and other assorted relatives, he handed Mrs. Breaux the pie. "Mrs. Mike sends this with her compliments," he said.

"Why, thank you very much, Jefferson. Your Mrs. Mike makes the best peach pie in all of south Louisiana, she does. You tell her I'll be sending her a little something come tomorrow morning, eh?" Angeline's mother looked from the pie to the package under his arm. "What else you got there?"

He shifted the paper-wrapped trousers and searched for an answer. To his surprise, Mrs. Breaux looked past him to offer up a broad smile.

"Now look who else is here." She handed off the pie to one of the elderly ladies with a brisk word of direction in French and clasped Jeff's hand. "Jefferson, I want you to meet Nicolas Arceneaux. Proper-like, that is."

Jeff whirled around to come face-to-face with the stranger he'd seen that morning. He stuck out his hand, and the Arceneaux fellow took it in a viselike grip.

"Pleased to meet you," Jeff said.

"Likewise." The stranger smiled and squeezed harder. "I didn't think you would come back."

For a moment Jeff stood mute, sizing up what he quickly decided was to be his competition. Strange he thought of that word, and yet as he studied the strapping Acadian, he felt exactly that.

"Now why wouldn't he come back, eh?" Clothilde asked. "You two boys go on inside and make merry with the rest of the family. How about that?"

"Actually I'd like to speak to this man a moment," the Acadian said. "If you don't mind, Mrs. Breaux."

Angeline's mother stared hard at him, then turned her gaze to Jeff. "Just a minute and not one second more, you hear?"

"Yes, Ma'am." He turned to Jeff. "Why don't you and I take a little walk?"

The challenge in his words was unmistakable. "Fine," Jeff said.

He looked down at the package beneath Jeff's arm. "Do you want to leave that here?"

Jeff leveled a hard stare. "Do I need to?"

The Acadian instantly backed away and smiled. "Not unless you want to."

Jeff let the statement hang between them just long enough to see the bigger man square his shoulders. "I suppose it doesn't matter, does it?"

"We're not talking about the package anymore, are we?"

To his surprise, the Arceneaux fellow clapped him on the shoulder and began to walk toward the edge of the clearing. "Ah, you are a smart man, are you not, Dr. Villare?" He did not wait for an answer. "I know this because we first talk about that package there, but then we begin to talk about my Angeline. You know this too."

"*Your* Angeline?" The question slipped out before Jeff could stop it.

The big man smiled. "Actually, yes."

His temper flared. How dare the big oaf assume any proprietary relationship with *his* Angeline? "Would you care to be more specific, Arceneaux?"

Instead of giving him an answer, Nicolas Arceneaux laughed. Jeff notched up his anger and took a step forward.

"There you are." Clothilde Breaux appeared at the edge of the clearing. "I have been looking all over for you."

She stared at Jefferson, then turned her attention to Nicolas. "Have you made friends with our Jefferson? He's practically like one of my own, you know. Why, his daddy and my daddy go way back. His daddy or Doc Broussard birthed every baby I had including my Angeline."

When neither responded, Mrs. Breaux linked arms with both men and turned toward the house. "Let's us go see the family, eh?" she said as she led them across the lawn and onto the porch.

Jeff stepped over the threshold behind Clothilde and allowed himself to be drawn into the boisterous crowd of Breaux family members. When he left, he knew he would leave a little piece of his heart beneath the patched roof of this cabin beside the Nouvelle. While he stayed, he would wonder what Nicolas Arceneaux meant.

The Acadian pressed past the crowd to meet Theophile Breaux in a serious conversation. A few moments later, Clothilde joined them and seemed to lighten their moods. At least she had them smiling until she walked away.

Meanwhile, Jeff made polite conversation with a distant cousin of Clothilde's, keeping a safe distance from Theophile and Arceneaux, who now huddled in the corner casting him furtive glances. Suddenly Angeline appeared in the room, stopping his heart and insuring that it would be left at her feet forever.

Flushed despite the relative cool of the May evening, she wore a pretty frock of pale green dotted with yellow rosebuds. Her thick hair had been captured and pinned in a knot at the base of her neck, the severe style only serving to emphasize her beautiful face. Dare he hope this show of beauty was for him?

Jeff rose from his seat by the fire to watch her float toward him. The room tunneled and closed until only the two of them occupied its space.

He took a step toward her, then froze as her father caught her by the elbow and tugged her over to join his conversation with the stranger. Angeline spared him only the slightest backward glance of regret before turning her attention to the men.

A familiar voice called his name. With difficulty, he tore his gaze from Angeline.

"Jefferson, welcome." Ernest Breaux grasped his hand in a hearty greeting and laughed. "So you're braver than I thought, eh?"

Braver? Foolish seemed a more apt description.

He thrust the package toward Ernest. "Say, Mrs. Mike sent this to Angeline. Would you see that she gets it later?"

"Sure," he said as he tossed the bundle onto the top of the old cypress pie safe. "Now tell me what's new with you."

"I'd rather hear what's new with you, Ernest. I'm afraid my life's terribly boring."

As Ernest began to regale him with his latest adventure working his father's traps, Jeff cast covert glances at Angeline.

When she smiled, he wondered why, and when she laughed, he longed to be in on the joke. But when her hand rose to her lips, shaking fingers pressed against her mouth, something turned to lead in his stomach. The stranger, he'd said something that caused her reaction. Was it good, this surprise, or terrible? From the high color on Angeline's cheeks, Jeff could not say.

seven

Ernest once more clapped a hand on Jeff's shoulder and drew him aside. "Why the long face, My Friend? The food is plentiful and the company good."

Jeff shrugged out of the smaller man's grasp. *And yet I have eyes only for. . .* The sound of laughter, Angeline's laughter, stopped him, and he had to clear his thoughts. "So when do we eat?"

"It is too long since you had the gumbo, eh? Well, you'll not eat like this for a long time, I understand," he said. "The word in town is that you'll be gone in two weeks."

"Actually, I'm expected to report for work in New York on the fifteenth, but I've got train tickets for Wednesday. I'd rather get settled before I start work."

Ernest's eyes narrowed. "Then why you nosing around my sister, eh? And I don't mean Mathilde."

He pondered several brilliant answers and gave up. *J'aurais pas du de venire me fourer ici.*

"You're probably right. You *shouldn't* have come here, but yet here you are, eh?"

Ernest touched Jeff's sleeve and gestured toward the tight group of people gathered around Theophile and the stranger. Only Angeline seemed to ignore the conversation and allow her gaze to flit around the room. A second later she noticed his stare and offered a shy smile before returning her attention to some anecdote Theophile was sharing.

"And little Angie," Ernest continued, "she looks to be happy you're here. Why, I haven't seen her wear that pretty dress since old man Fouchet married the youngest of the

47

Viator girls last January. No, she didn't get herself prettied up for nothing, and I would bet my best pirogue it's not for that fellow Papa brought home."

Something like hope coiled inside Jeff, and he almost asked Ernest to repeat the statement. Instead, he shook his head. "Angeline and I are friends, Ernest, you know that."

"Some say more than friends, eh?"

So there it was again, the old rumor that he and the beautiful Angeline had allowed their passion to find action. Would it never die?

"What we have just goes beyond good sense, I guess, but it *never* went where the gossips claimed."

"*Sa fini pas.*"

Jeff jerked his attention toward Ernest. "That's what your father said. 'The thing that never ends.' Yes," he said with a wry chuckle, "I will admit that just might be the best way to put what your sister and I share. Ah, but it is bittersweet, My Friend. She was meant to stay here, and I was meant to leave. What is the point of dwelling on it?"

Ernest looked thoughtful for a moment. "Do you love her?"

"*Sa fait pas rien.*"

"Oh, but it does matter."

"Monsieur Jefferson." Jeff felt a light touch on his sleeve and turned to stare into the wide brown eyes of Mathilde Breaux. "Perhaps you could help me with a few things in the kitchen? I find my strength is just about gone, and the gumbo pot is quite heavy to lift tonight."

She did look a bit pale, and delicate smudges of charcoal shadowed her eyes. Still, he saw mischief on her face. "Perhaps your brother might—"

"Ernest, get over here an' tell this good man about that ole three-legged gator we done saw last week," Theophile called.

"Looks like you're elected, My Friend," Ernest said as he turned his back and headed toward his father.

Jeff reluctantly allowed himself to be dragged across the room and into the starry night toward the summer kitchen. Clothilde shouted a warning to one of the little ones as they strolled past the window. "I'm going to check the gumbo for Angie, Mama," Mathilde called. She giggled when her mother responded with a complaint about her sister's forgetfulness tonight. "I don't mind, really." She gave Jeff a wink.

Jeff took in a deep breath of damp air and let it out slowly. This evening was not going as he had planned. Perhaps he should forget about Angeline and her gumbo and take his leave. A wise man knew when to cut his losses. Isn't that what Pop always said?

He watched Mathilde lift the lid on the iron pot and reach for the long metal spoon hanging on a hook beside the stove. The aroma of gumbo wafted toward him, and he inhaled deeply. "That smells good," he said as he watched her stir the thick brown roux.

"I've been wondering something, Monsieur Jefferson," Mathilde said as she reached for a canister and added something to the mixture.

"What's that?"

"Nothing." She dipped a small spoon into the pot, then held it to her lips to blow away the steam. "Taste this to see if it's ready."

It was heavenly. Every bit as good as he remembered. Jeff nodded. "Definitely ready."

"Good. I'll tell Mama." Mathilde dropped the spoon into the wash bucket, then swayed a second before grasping the corner of the stove.

Jeff steadied her. "Are you all right?"

She turned to face him and offered a weak smile. "Of course I'm fine." She looked past him, and he followed her gaze to stare at the house. A sliver of yellow light danced across the yard, chased by the laughter and voices of the people inside.

"Angie loves it here," she whispered. "This is her home."

He nodded and pushed away the sadness that went along with this truth. "Yes, it is."

"She will never leave this place, you know?"

Jeff leaned against the rough wooden wall and stared into the window, hoping to catch a glimpse of Angeline. "I know," he said softly. "I've always known that."

"This question I wanted to ask, it is difficult and personal. May I still ask?"

"Well, I don't know." He cast a glance at her and saw she was serious. "Of course."

"Do you love her?"

Jeff chuckled and continued to watch for Angeline's face at the window. "Is that all? Would it make you feel better to know you're not the first person to ask me that today?"

"It might," Mathilde said in a weak voice. "What was your answer?"

Before he could respond, Mathilde fainted.

❧

The last thing Angeline expected Jefferson to carry through the door was her sister Mathilde. As the crowd parted and allowed the doctor to deposit her on the settee, Angeline drew near.

Mama pushed her away to press her palm against Mathilde's brow. "She looks a bit flushed," she said. "You think it's the heat or something else, Jefferson?"

"I'm not sure. Let me have a look at her."

Jeff knelt at Mathilde's side and cradled her hand in his as he listened to her pulse. Mathilde's eyelids fluttered open. "What happened?" she whispered.

"You had another dizzy spell, *Bebe,*" Mama directed her attention to Jefferson. "That's the second time today my girl done fell off her feets. This morning I thought she was gone fall right into the baby's bathwater."

"Why didn't you tell me none of this, Clothilde?" Theophile

demanded. "A man ought to know what goes on in his own house, eh?"

"How long have you been feeling dizzy, Mathilde?" Jefferson asked.

"Just today, I suppose."

"Then maybe it's nothing, eh?" Mama asked as she gave Jefferson a hopeful look. "Our little Amalie, she down wit the fever, but she don't got the dizzies. You think they might have caught the same thing, my girls?"

"I say we call a real doctor," Theophile shouted.

"Hush now." Mama gave Papa a look she generally reserved for the worst behaved of the little ones. "What's wrong with my *bebe*, Jefferson? Can you tell?"

Jeff shook his head. "Could be nothing that a good meal and a night's rest won't cure." He paused. "I don't detect a fever, but should one arise, that would definitely be a cause for concern. As for Amalie, I recommend you watch her for signs of change. I assume she's resting tonight."

Mama nodded. "She was tired, so I put her to bed early. What are you thinking? You don't think this is the bad fever, no?"

Angeline could see the panic in Mama's eyes. They both remembered the influenza epidemic of Angeline's childhood, the one that started so innocently and ended with the deaths of far too many.

"I'm thinking this is probably nothing, Mrs. Breaux, so don't worry just yet." He addressed Mathilde. "How are you feeling now?"

She struggled to sit upright. "I'm a little shaky, but I'll be fine." She batted her eyes. "Maybe it was just the company."

Theophile shook his head. "I think all she needs is some good gumbo in her. Angie, go fetch the pot. Nicolas, would you mind helping my girl? I'm afraid the pot's a might heavy for her."

Banished, Angeline strode toward the summer kitchen not caring whether the stranger followed or not. In her current frame of mind, she could have carried two gumbo pots to Latanier and back, much less one to the long table just inside the front door.

She stomped past Mama's Easter lilies and ducked under the low branch of the magnolia on the corner of the house. If Papa's stranger was behind her, he'd definitely glimpsed a less than ladylike side of her.

Convicted of her rudeness, she slowed her pace and cast a glance over her shoulder. To her surprise, Nicolas had kept up with her and now tagged only a step behind.

"Do you always move this fast?" he asked when their gazes met.

"I'm sorry," she said. "My mind was on other things."

"I see." He ducked his head. "I feel as though we ought to visit a bit alone, Mademoiselle Breaux. Would you mind?"

"Of course not." Angeline took a step backward and leaned against the corner of the house. Under other circumstances, she might have found him quite pleasing to the eye. Tonight, she only had eyes for a certain doctor.

"I suppose you're wondering why I'm here." He paused. "Or maybe you're not."

She cast about for something to change the direction of the conversation. "Papa speaks very highly of you. I understand you are a fisherman."

"I am." He met her gaze with eyes that seemed to study her intently. "As my father before me and his before him. It's not an easy life, but it is a good one."

"I see."

He grasped her hand with work-roughened fingers that felt like Papa's. "I know this is sudden, but—"

She broke from his touch and turned toward the kitchen. *"Allons!* The gumbo needs bringing inside."

"Don't be afraid," he whispered. "I know it is not me you love." Nicolas caught her elbow and whirled her around. "I saw how you looked at that city fellow."

All she could do was stare. What in the world did he intend by bringing up something such as that? "What business is that of yours?"

He shook his head. "I may be just a bayou boy, but I'm not dumb. If you keep company with that man, you're going to hurt more than just your mama and papa."

"Honestly, I don't know what you're talking about. Now can we just go back inside?"

Nicolas tightened his grip. "Tonight you will seek the Lord, eh? *Le Bon Dieu,* He will tell you what to do about this problem you will be having."

"What problem are you talking about?" Angeline stared at the big Acadian. She looked past him to the stand of trees and thought of the bayou beyond, how it flowed at will and bowed to no man. "The only problem I have right now is you."

eight

As soon as she said the words, she wanted to reel them back in. What had gotten into her tonight? More to the point, what had gotten into her all day?

Of course, the answer to that question stood just inside the cabin door. Seeing Jefferson Villare had turned her day—and her whole world—upside down.

"Let's just bring in the gumbo and forget we had this conversation, Monsieur Arceneaux."

"Call me Nicolas, please, and I will call you Angeline, eh?" He released her to touch her chin with his thumb and guided her attention back to his. "I'll get straight to the point."

"The point?"

"*Oui*. I will treat you like a queen, Mademoiselle. I will love you like the Lord requires a husband to love his wife."

Wife. Angeline stifled an indelicate gulp. Until this moment, the reality of her situation had only danced at the edge of her mind. With Jefferson Villare so near, how could she determine tonight to pledge her life to another?

And yet, if Papa insisted on it, how could she not?

"Please let us not talk of these things tonight." She walked toward the gumbo pot and worked the spoon through the thick brown roux.

Nicolas removed the spoon from her hand and placed it on the hook. Once again, he enveloped her hand with his. "Your man, he will be gone soon and you will forget him. Then where will you be?"

The look he gave her stilled her tongue and kept her cry of denial from becoming words. She allowed her shoulders to slump. Forget Jefferson Villare? Never. Admit to that? Also never.

"I say this not to hurt you, but to show you the logic of things as they are between my family and yours."

"The logic of things?" She shook her head. "What does logic have to do with anything?"

A smile brightened his face. The change, and its resulting effect, was dazzling. Angeline averted her gaze, startled.

"Ah, now you ask a question I can answer." He once again placed his thumb beneath her chin and directed her to look into his eyes. "You are a smart woman, eh? A woman who understands how things are."

"I don't know what you mean."

"Come, let's sit." He indicated the rough bench Papa and Ernest had made last winter, now nestled beneath the branches of the flowering magnolia. When she settled beside him, he rested his elbows on his knees and let out a sigh. "Your papa and my papa, they strike a deal, Angeline."

"A deal?" She batted at an errant mosquito. "What do you mean?"

"You and me, we're the deal."

Angeline stood. "I don't know what you're talking about, but I do know that Mama will come looking for both of us if we don't fetch the gumbo to the table."

Her companion gently pulled her back down beside him. "My papa, he was in a bad way, and he needed a pirogue and some skins, a little wood for the winter fire, and a little money for the summer fishing. Your papa, well, he needed. . ." His voice faded and disappeared against the chirp of the crickets.

Humiliation drove her to finish his sentence. "He needed a husband for his *vielle fille*, his old maid daughter."

Nicolas wrapped an arm around her shoulder. "No, hush now, that's not what he said." He paused. "I probably shouldn't tell you what he *did* say though."

"Why?" She looked at him. He did have the nicest smile.

"Because I'm afraid it might go to your head." He nudged her shoulder with his. "It wouldn't do for you to think you're the most beautiful belle on the bayou."

The sentiment took her breath away. "Papa said that?"

"No," Nicolas said slowly, "I did." He straightened his shoulders and stood, then offered her a hand to pull her up beside him. He held her hand for a moment. "Your papa, he merely said you were very pretty. Now perhaps we should keep your family waiting no longer."

"My family?"

Again, he offered that smile. "*Oui*, Angeline, they are waiting for the gumbo, eh?"

"The gumbo. *Oui.*"

How foolish she felt as she followed Nicolas inside, carrying the smaller pot of rice while he easily bore the burden of the iron gumbo pot. After setting the rice on the table, she turned to her mother while Nicolas allowed Papa to lead him away.

Her mother leaned close. "How you like Papa's friend, *Bebe*?"

"He's nice enough," she said.

A raised eyebrow served as her mother's response before she bustled off to supervise the setting of the table. Angeline joined her.

When Papa tugged on her arm and pulled her aside, Angeline's heart sank. Standing with him was Nicolas Arceneaux.

"Nicolas, he told me he talked to you," Papa said. When she nodded, he said, "Good, then tonight we make the announcement, eh?"

Angeline froze. "Please, Papa, no."

Papa gave Nicolas a confused look. "She don't look like you talked to her."

"I did, Sir," Nicolas said. "Maybe I didn't talk plain enough."

"Then make it plain, eh?"

Please, Lord, don't let this happen. You know I don't love this man.

Nicolas reached for Angeline's hand. "Angeline Breaux, will you be my wedded wife?"

"Angie, Sweetheart," her mother called, "where's the gumbo ladle?"

"The ladle?" She reached behind her to pick up a dish towel and look beneath it, anything to distract Papa and Nicolas from this conversation. "I thought we had it. Check the gumbo pot. Maybe it fell inside."

"It's not there. Did you leave it in the summer kitchen?"

"I'll go look."

Angeline slipped out the door and headed for the summer kitchen, moving across the lawn at a fast pace. The sounds of the night rang in her ears, along with the memory of her conversation with Nicolas.

Did he tell the truth? Had Papa really promised her hand in marriage to a fisherman just to keep her close to home? Even if his intentions had been good, how could Papa sell her like a prize pig to the highest bidder?

No answers came, so she turned to the Lord as she stalked toward the little kitchen. Even He seemed to be silent.

Once inside the summer kitchen, Angeline found the ladle hanging on the hook beside the stove and grabbed it. "How could we have forgotten this?" she muttered.

Because you were too busy discussing marriage.

Clutching the ladle, she stepped outside and took a deep breath. The sooner the food was served, the sooner the night would end. Better to hurry than tarry.

Of course, if she tarried, Nicolas might not have time to ask her to marry him. She shook her head. It didn't matter. If Papa intended her to wed Nicolas, all the time in the world wouldn't change his mind.

If only Jefferson weren't here to witness the announcement.

As she rushed back toward the house, she turned the corner

to race up the porch and ran headlong into Jefferson Villare. The ladle fell and she nearly tumbled after it.

"Slow down there," he whispered as he helped her upright.

"I'm sorry, I wasn't watching where I was going." She took a step backward to pick up the ladle and wipe it off on the front of her skirt. "Mama will have my hide for getting this dirty."

Even in the shadows, she could see the twinkle in his eyes. Oh, but he did look handsome all dressed up in his Sunday clothes!

Don't look at him. You can't. You're about to become engaged, and he's leaving.

"I doubt that," he said in a husky voice. "You could talk your mama out of being mad every time."

Angeline chuckled despite herself and shook her head. "I think you must have me confused with someone else."

His gaze turned from amused to tender, and he reached out to touch her cheek with his hand. "I assure you that would never happen."

Without thinking, she placed her hand over his and leaned into his embrace. A moment later, he kissed her.

Unlike the kiss they shared earlier in the day, this one was sweet and soft and could have gone on forever if Mama hadn't appeared at the door.

To her credit, Mama said nothing but rather removed the ladle from Angeline's fingers and stepped back inside. She did make eye contact with Angeline as she passed by the window. There would be some serious talking between the two of them tomorrow—that much was certain.

There would also be some serious talking with the Lord tonight.

Angeline held the back of her hand against her lips and averted her gaze. Heat flamed her face, and her fingers trembled slightly.

"We shouldn't have done that," she whispered.

"And yet we just can't seem to stop."

"But we can't just keep—" Jefferson leaned closer and gave her another quick kiss, silencing her words as he enveloped her in an embrace.

"All right, everybody," Mama called, "the gumbo's ready. Set yourselves at the table and get ready for some good eatin', eh?"

"We can't ever do that again, Jefferson," she said as she leaned her head on his shoulder.

"Why?" he whispered against her ear.

"Because Papa has other plans for me."

Jefferson held her at arm's length and gave her a confused look. "What are you talking about, Angeline? What plans?"

Try as she might, she couldn't find the words to tell him her father had promised her to another man. Instead, she broke free and darted inside, unsure if her legs could carry her as far as the table.

What Jefferson did not know now, he would most likely find out by the end of the night. Papa and Nicolas had been thick as thieves most of the evening. To her mind, that meant one or both of them would be delivering the news that a wedding was afoot, even if she hadn't given Nicolas a proper answer to his proposal.

Busying herself with serving duties, she did not see Jefferson slip inside, but he must have, for she looked up to see him standing next to Mathilde. Her sister laughed at something Jefferson said, then touched his hand, and the green monster of envy hit Angeline.

As soon as she recognized the feeling for what it was, she pushed it away. Maybe the Lord meant for Jefferson to find happiness with the younger of the two Breaux women. Perhaps that was why He led him back to their doorstep.

If only she could muster some enthusiasm for the idea. But with the young doctor's kisses still warm on her lips, Angeline could find nothing good about encouraging such a relationship.

No, if she couldn't have Jefferson Villare, then it would be best that he just leave. Having him as a brother-in-law would be the worst possible thing.

"Go set yourself, Girlie," Papa called. "The food's gettin' cold and I'm gettin' old a-waitin'."

"Yes, Papa," she said as she forced her attention in his direction.

Fortunately he gave no indication of having noticed that she'd been staring at Jefferson. Unfortunately, when she turned her gaze to Nicolas, who stood beside Papa, she knew for sure that *he* had.

While Mama bundled the little ones off to their own smaller table in the corner, Papa took his seat at the head of the big table and instructed Nicolas to sit on his right. Mathilde settled in the chair on his left. Jefferson was ordered to deposit himself in the spot beside her.

Somehow, when all those in attendance were seated, there was only one place left at the table for Angeline—next to Nicolas and across from Jefferson. Mathilde rested happily next to the young doctor, her silliness already apparent in the way she monopolized the conversation with him.

Angeline's gaze met Mama's, and she cringed when her mother's eyes narrowed. Should she raise a fuss about the awkward seating arrangement, Mama would say something for sure. Rather than risk yet another embarrassment, Angeline meekly slipped into the spot next to Nicolas and bowed her head while Papa prayed.

As her father offered up thanks for the meal and a blessing for those in attendance, Angeline added a silent prayer of her own. *Please, Lord, get me through this evening.*

nine

Please, Lord, get me through this evening.

Jefferson added an "amen" to the chorus, then held out his bowl for white rice and gumbo. He tried in vain to catch Angeline's attention, but she seemed inordinately interested in the elderly maiden aunt seated beside her. At least that conversation kept her from talking to the Arceneaux fellow.

The discussion also kept him, at least in part, from thinking about the kisses he shared with Angeline. Still, as the sweet elderly lady droned on about chickens and eggs, he drifted back to those few blissful moments on the porch when time had fallen backwards and he and Angeline hadn't a care in the world.

"Are you listening, Young Man?"

"Oh, I'm sorry," he said as he forced his attention back to the present.

Half an hour later, he'd dropped his spoon three times, allowed a sizable shrimp and some roux to land on his trousers, and spilled rice down the front of his shirt. He finally gave up when Angeline's father caught him picking rice out of his pocket.

During the entire time, Angeline did not look at him once. Had she not been as moved by their kiss—actually, kisses—as he? Surely she had, for he'd seen the look on her face before she fled.

As long as he lived he would never forget that look.

He neatly tucked the fluffy white grains under his napkin and attempted to pay attention to a loud conversation between Ernest and the Acadian. He did all this despite the constant flow of words from Mathilde, to his right.

His mind wandered and so did his gaze. Both landed on Angeline.

Silhouetted in the lamplight, she now gave her complete attention to the fisherman as he told another story, the topic of which totally escaped Jeff. When Mathilde's elbow collided with his rib, he nearly knocked his plate of peach pie off the table. Recovering with an embarrassed grin toward the incredulous Mr. Breaux, he ignored Angeline's stare to turn his attention to her younger sister.

Even in the yellow light of the kerosene lamp, he could see her skin was pale and the dark smudges beneath her eyes had deepened. The doctor in him sounded a warning, while the man in him wanted to voice his irritation. Instead, he remained silent as she leaned toward him.

"The last thing you want Papa to know is how much you care for my sister," she whispered.

He cast a quick glance at Mr. Breaux, who was now heavily involved in a debate over water rights with the fisherman. "I don't know what you're talking about."

"You're looking like a lovesick puppy, Jefferson Villare, and everyone in this room except Papa and Angie has noticed." She punctuated the statement with an innocent smile, then dabbed at the corner of her mouth with her napkin. "Once Papa notices, I'm sure he'll speed up the wedding just to save Angie from the likes of you."

"Wedding? What wedding?" Jeff knew he'd spoken too loud when all conversation at the table ceased.

Mathilde dropped her napkin into her lap and broadened her smile. "We were talking about Sissy Fontenot's big Christmas wedding. Jefferson here didn't realize little Sissy had gone and got married without sending him an invitation. They were practically neighbors, you know."

"Well, how about that, eh?" Mrs. Breaux chimed in. A

moment later, the various members of the Breaux clan were buzzing with their memories of what must have been the wedding of the century.

The only two people not participating in the conversation were Jeff and Nicolas Arceneaux. Jeff gave the intruder a direct look, sizing up his competition, and Arceneaux seemed to do the same. Without breaking eye contact, the fisherman quirked a corner of his mouth into a smile and placed a hand on Angeline's sleeve. As she turned her attention to him, Jefferson pushed away from the table.

"Excuse me, folks, but I really must leave."

"Sit down, Young Man." Theophile Breaux's voice echoed in the room, bouncing off wooden walls to land square in Jeff's gut. "Nobody goes anywhere just yet. I got somethin' to say."

≈

Angeline nearly jumped out of her chair when Papa turned his attention to her. Nicolas removed his hand from her arm and rested it around the back of her chair.

All through dinner, she'd expected Nicolas to repeat the question she hadn't answered. When he did not, she'd felt some relief. Now that relief turned to stone in her throat.

Obviously Papa and the groom were going on with the wedding plans even if the bride hadn't yet said she would attend.

"What's this about, eh?" Clothilde asked as she dropped her napkin onto the table. "You running for mayor or somethin', Theophile? 'Cause if you are, you don't have to make no speeches in this house, no. We would all vote for you, now wouldn't we?"

Peals of laughter erupted at the comment until Papa held up his hand to bring order to the room. "Now you just go and be funny some other time and place, Cleo, why don't you? Can't a man be serious in his own home?"

Mama hid a smile behind her hand as she nodded. "Of

course you can, Dear. Please, don't let me interrupt. Go ahead with what you were going to say."

Papa cleared his throat and stood, placing his palms on the table. "We all had some good gumbo tonight, eh?"

When the cries of agreement from those settled around the table died down, Papa spoke again. "Well, my girl Angeline, she made that gumbo. She's a right good cook and she helps her mama with the babies too." He slapped Nicolas on the shoulder. "She'll make a man a good wife someday, eh?"

"*Oui*, Monsieur Breaux," Nicholas said as he gave her a brief but admiring look. "She will indeed."

Waves of embarrassment washed over Angeline. Surely Papa didn't intend to announce her wedding, not in front of Jefferson.

"Goodness, Papa, now you're making it sound like Angie's running for office," Mathilde said with a giggle.

"Lord, please deliver me from the females in my home," Papa muttered as he glared at Mathilde. "Now, as I was tryin' t' say—"

"Mama! Angie!" Amalie's plaintive cry interrupted her father's words. "I'm thirsty."

"I'll see to her." Angeline jumped up and raced toward the back bedroom with a cup of water, not waiting for an answer.

"Angie, tell me a story," the little girl whispered. "I want to hear the one about T-Boy the gator and his friend Redfish."

"A little later, maybe," she said. Right now she couldn't tell a story if her life depended on it. Her mind, such as it was, held only one thought, and it had nothing to do with a fictional alligator and his fishy friend.

As she held the cup to her little sister's lips, she gave thanks for the small reprieve she'd been granted. Just in case Papa decided to try again, Angeline nudged Amalie over a bit and climbed into bed beside her. If anyone came looking for her, they would find her asleep—or at least pretending to be asleep.

And while that might only delay the inevitable by a day, it might also give God time to act. What He would do was a mystery, but surely He didn't intend for her to be wed to a stranger.

❧

A moment later, with Theophile Breaux distracted, Jeff made all the appropriate gestures of gratitude to Clothilde and made his escape. He got all the way to the car before he heard someone call his name. Praying he could still leave quickly, Jeff turned toward the feminine voice.

"Yes?"

Clothilde Breaux stood on the bottom step of the porch with a dark, round object in her hand. "Hold up there, Jefferson, eh?" she called as she began to cross the shadowed lawn.

His heart sank. If Mrs. Breaux insisted, he would stay all night. He couldn't possibly let the sweet woman down, but he also couldn't possibly spend another moment in the room with Angeline and the Acadian.

"Here, *Bebe*," she said as she thrust the dark object toward him. It was the covered pie plate, and she'd put something inside—it felt heavy and sloshed a bit. "You tell Mrs. Mike that was the best pie she's ever made."

"I'll do that," he said as he leaned over to set the plate on the floor of the car.

"I sent her a little gumbo. I know how she likes the shrimps, so I put her some extra in." Clothilde touched Jeff's sleeve. "You don't have to run off, you know. Uncle Joe, he's gone play his fiddle for us in a bit."

Jeff smiled. "I appreciate the offer, but I'm tired. I think I need to get back home."

Her smile didn't quite match his. In the moonlight, she looked so much like her daughter—older and wiser, to be sure, but none the less beautiful. How funny that she held her beauty and the inner peace that radiated around her, even though she'd never left the banks of the Nouvelle.

How could anyone be that happy in a place this small and stifling?

"I understand," she said. "Tell Mrs. Mike I've got her some Easter lilies ready to go."

"I will."

To his surprise, she winked. "And don't you worry about our Angie. God's got something special for her; I just know it. And you're gonna know it too, you'll see."

"What do you mean?"

Her smile grew. "Leave Angie's papa to me and the Lord. You pray to God about your problems, and He give you the solutions, eh?"

"I will," he said, although he had no idea what she meant.

As he drove away, he glanced back and watched the cabin fade in the shadows. He wondered: Was he destined always to remember this place in that way—as a comfortable spot that had faded to black?

All the way back into town, he thought about the Acadian's smile and his hand atop Angeline's.

The way Arceneaux huddled with Mr. Breaux indicated the two were in league with one another. Could Mathilde be correct? Did Angeline's papa intend to marry her off to Nicolas Arceneaux?

By the time he parked Pop's car and trudged up the back steps, he'd almost convinced himself that nothing Angeline Breaux did mattered anymore. He would have completed the process had he not been confronted by Mrs. Mike.

"Waiting up for me?" he asked with a grin.

"I wish that were the case," she said. "But Doc's been here twice looking for you. He left you this note."

She fished a piece of paper out of her pastel-striped house-coat and handed it to Jeff. Struggling to read the doctor's hand-writing, he finally deduced that he was needed at the clinic immediately. Something about having too many patients and not enough doctors.

Jeff groaned. When he agreed to help Doc, he hadn't actually expected he might be needed.

"Bad news?" she asked.

"I hope not." He handed her the pie tin. "Mrs. Breaux sends her thanks along with some shrimp gumbo and said for you to come see her. She's got some Easter lilies for you." He shucked off his tie. "Oh, and she said this was your best pie ever," he added as he rounded the corner toward the front foyer.

"How is Clothilde?" he heard Mrs. Mike ask.

"She's very well. Very well indeed."

"And Angeline?"

"Why don't you go on out there tomorrow and see for yourself?"

"I just might."

As Jeff took the stairs by twos, heading toward his room and a change of clothes, he could hear Mrs. Mike expounding on the virtues of the Breaux family. He strode past the bed and pulled a clean shirt out of the armoire. Thoughts of Angeline mingled with concern over the emergency that would keep him from much-needed sleep a bit longer.

When he arrived at the clinic, he saw the need for the urgency. Three families waited on the porch and four more sat inside. Each had at least one member exhibiting signs of the dreaded influenza.

Thoughts of Angeline Breaux fled as Jeff went to meet Doc in the exam room. Three hours later, the patients continued to trickle in, and Jeff had given up any idea of sleeping that night.

ten

Angeline stood beside the shed and watched Mama work at tending her precious bed of flowers. With the little ones taking a Monday morning nap and the others playing quietly, it was the perfect time to have a heart-to-heart talk with the one person in the world besides the Lord who knew her best.

Thankfully Nicolas had left after church yesterday to return to his fishing, and Papa and Ernest were out this morning in the pirogue. For a short while, she and Mama would be left alone to talk.

Grabbing a trowel from the peg on the wall, she strolled toward Mama and dropped down beside her. Mama gave her a smile, then went back to her weeding.

"Something on your mind, *Bebe?*" she asked without looking up from her task. "Maybe something to do with your intended, Mr. Arceneaux?"

"So Papa told you?"

"Of course he did. You don't think my Theophile can keep something like this from me, do you?" She paused. "Besides, the mama of the bride's got to make the plans, eh?"

"Bride," she said with a groan.

"Maybe you think you the only woman in love who is gonna get married, eh?"

Angeline stuck the trowel in the ground and crossed her arms over her chest. "I'm not in love, Mama. That's not the problem."

Mama stopped her work. "Then maybe you tell me what's the problem, eh?"

"Men, that's the problem." Angeline shook her head. "Why do they all have to think they are the only ones with

68

an opinion? And why is it that when we have an opinion, no one asks us for it?"

"And yet this don't have *nothing* to do with love?"

"No, Mama," she said, "it has to do with Papa."

Her mother smiled. "Now that's a subject I know a little about. Why don't you and me go get a cool drink of water and sit over there in the shade and talk about your papa, eh?"

Angeline stood and helped her mother to her feet. Together they walked in step toward the well. While Angeline poured two dipperfuls of water into tin cups, Mama settled on the bench beneath the magnolia.

"I am forever grateful to your papa and brother for making me this little resting bench," she said as she accepted the cup from Angeline. "It does a body good to sit a spell when you're tired, eh?" She shook her head. "But we were talking about your papa. What is it he's done this time, *Bebe?*"

"You know what he's done, Mama." She took a furious gulp of water. "He's gone and sold me off to the highest bidder against my will. That's what he's done."

Mama seemed to contemplate the statement a moment. "And you said this had nothing to do with love."

Angeline fairly jumped off the bench. "It doesn't! Papa never asked me if I loved Nicolas Arceneaux, and he certainly didn't ask me if I wanted to marry him."

"And if he had, what would you have said?" Angeline's silence must have spoken for her, for Mama began to smile. "You're just like me, you know? You love a man, and you love him forever. That's how it is with me and your papa."

Angeline settled back beside Mama and took her hand. "How did you know, Mama? What told you Papa was the one?"

Mama patted Angeline's hand. "Not what, *Bebe*, but Who. God—He told me your papa was the one."

"Well so far, God's not the one making decisions around here, is He?" Since Mama looked like she was about to launch into one of her lectures about God always being in control, Angeline pressed forward with her point. "See, Mama, Papa's making all the decisions. He's not even bothering to ask me."

"But do you know whether he's bothering to ask God? That's the real question, eh?" Mama sighed. "Do you know why your papa picked Nicolas Arceneaux for you?"

She nodded. "Nicolas told me Papa made a deal with his father, something about furs and other things."

"That's only a part of it, Angie."

"So you admit that Papa traded me like a pile of furs?"

"No, I admit nothing of the sort." Inside the house, the baby began to fret. Mama stood and stretched her back. "What I'm trying to tell you is that Papa picked Nicolas Arceneaux for a reason, and it has nothing to do with the fact that his papa needed some furs for the winter."

Mama tossed the remains of her water into the flowerbed and returned the cup to its place at the well. Angeline followed suit, then tagged behind her mother as she trudged toward the steps. "I'll get her, Mama. You just rest here."

After the baby had been changed and returned to Mama to nurse, Angeline broached the subject of marriage once more. "Mama, will you tell me why you think Papa sold me off to the Arceneaux family?"

Mama toyed with the baby's dark hair and looked off into the distance. "The bayou, she is a beautiful thing, eh? For a man or woman of proud Acadian birth, she is our life." She looked to Angeline for confirmation.

"*Oui,*" she said.

"And this place, this is our home. We have deep roots here, *Bebe.* Your papa's people and mine, they come to settle this place two hundred years ago, eh?"

"Yes, Mama."

Her mother's dark eyes flashed anger. "Then why would

your papa allow his precious girl to leave her roots and her home? Why lose his *bebe* when there is a godly man who promises not to take her away?"

"Mama, what are you talking about?"

Mama lifted the baby to her shoulder and began rubbing circles on her little back. "I'm talking about love and marriage, Angie, same as you."

Angeline leaned against the porch post and tried to make sense of the conversation. Why would Papa think she might leave home if she wasn't married off to the likes of Nicolas Arceneaux? She never even considered the idea.

But she had considered what it would be like to marry Jefferson Villare, hadn't she?

"A penny for your thoughts, Angie."

"You and Papa have nothing to worry about, you know," she said with a sigh. "There never was anything between Jefferson and me besides a friendship. I thought you believed me."

With her free hand, Mama lifted Angeline's chin and offered a smile. "I never did doubt. I know my girl's a good girl and I know Jefferson; he's a good boy." She paused. "But I know love when I see it, and I know Jefferson thinks he's not meant to stay. Marry up with him, and he'll take you where you'll never see home again."

"Is that what this is about? Papa thinks I'm going to marry Jefferson if he doesn't find someone else for me?" She pounded her fists on her knees. "Why can't he just let me be? I promise I'm not going anywhere. You need me here to help, and I don't care if I ever get married."

Again Mama shook her head. "That is the anger talking, *Bebe*. Even if you don't know you love him, I do and so does your papa. God knows too. You mark my words, though. You stand too close to the fire that young doctor's got burning inside him, and you gonna get burned."

A wail went up from inside the house. It was the twins,

crying in unison. "Mama," one said. "Make Amalie wake up," the other finished.

"Oh, I hope that precious child's not sick again. I thought we had her well."

Angeline placed a hand on Mama's shoulder. "See, you need me here. I'll handle this. Likely as not, Amalie's playing possum so she doesn't have to help Mathilde take care of the babies."

But when she found her sister lying on the settee, she knew Amalie was not playing possum. The little girl was burning up with fever.

"Mama, come here, please!" Angeline shouted. "Something's wrong with Amalie."

Mama handed the baby to Angeline and knelt beside Amalie. "Oh, *Bebe*, I'm gonna pray this isn't what I think it is." She looked up at Angeline. "Put the baby in her bed, and go fetch the doctor. I don't think we can get her to the office without Papa or the boys here. You tell him this is urgent, you hear, eh?"

"Yes, Mama."

Angeline found her way to the old pirogue Papa kept around for the children and began to paddle furiously toward town. By the time she reached the docks, her fingers were raw and her back was soaked with sweat. Tying up the boat despite the pain in her hands, she set off toward Doc Broussard's office only to find a note on the door stating that he was out seeing patients. The message referred all emergencies to Jefferson Villare.

Angeline knew all too well how to find Jefferson's home, and she returned to her pirogue to trace the winding path of the bayou until it reached the Villare place. In her mind, she'd always thought of the big house as a mansion. When Papa would read the verse in the Bible about God's house having many mansions, she always pictured Jefferson's house. Funny how her age had changed, but her perspective had remained the same.

Even now as she trudged toward the big double front doors and the wide porch filled with white rocking chairs, she felt like the teenager she'd been the last time she walked across the threshold. She'd often wondered if their last day together, the day Doc Villare had come home to find his son and the poor Acadian girl alone in the big house, had really changed the course of two lives, or whether it just seemed that way looking back.

The moment had been as innocent as they were, just two friends sharing Mrs. Mike's peach pie across the kitchen table. As far as they knew, Mrs. Mike was somewhere in the house rather than out running errands for the afternoon. Angeline had never contemplated what Doc Villare accused them of doing—at least not seriously. The end result was the same. Two reputations tarnished and a pair of good friends separated.

As long as she lived, she would always wonder whether what happened that afternoon was part of God's plan or Satan's.

eleven

"I'm sorry, but he's unavailable right now."

The sound of his housekeeper's voice danced at the edge of Jeff's favorite dream, the one where he and Angeline sat on the banks of the Nouvelle dipping their toes in the warm water and frightening away any fish they thought to catch. They couldn't have been more than ten or twelve, and he, the city boy, had boasted an ability to catch fish well beyond his capacity to do so.

True to her gentle and understanding nature, Angeline suggested it would be much more fun to see who could kick water the farthest.

He won that contest; he always did.

The dream abruptly changed course, and he and Angeline were seated at the kitchen table, a peach pie and two glasses of milk between them.

Jeff shifted in Pop's chair and allowed his body to relax once more. He'd worked two days and two nights straight, with only a few hours of stolen sleep on Doc's office couch in the process. When the number of influenza cases slowed to a manageable level and the house calls began, Doc sent him home. He'd gone willingly, he was ashamed to say, but he'd promised to get some rest and return in the afternoon. In the meantime, Doc promised to send someone to fetch him if things got out of hand again.

Jeff edged down into the chair and rested his chin on his chest. Just a few more minutes of sleep, a few more minutes reliving the past, and he would make the trek upstairs to his room and a real bed for sure.

Just a few more minutes. . .

"But you don't understand," a female voice said in his dream. "It's my sister; she's sick with a fever. Papa and Ernest are gone, so Mama sent me to town to fetch a doctor."

Fever. Doctor. Those words had no place in his dream.

Shaking the cobwebs from his brain, Jeff rose and stretched his complaining muscles. Too many hours bending over an exam table and too little sleep had left him feeling twice his age. How did Pop and Doc manage to attend to an endless line of patients, day after day, week after week, with no attention to schedules or office hours?

At least the life of a research physician offered regular hours and stools that didn't cause back strain. *Yes, but what of the looks of gratitude on the faces of parents or the reward in knowing a life had been saved?*

Jeff shook off the question. Many parents would be grateful and many lives would be saved by the eradication of influenza. He should be thankful God chose him to be a part of medical research, rather than spend his time wondering if he'd misunderstood the Lord's leading.

Bright shafts of sunlight pushed through the windows and formed a pattern on the old Persian rug. Dust motes danced in the light. The clock on the mantle read a few minutes before noon.

The best he could tell, he'd been asleep in Pop's chair for nearly five hours. No wonder he was so stiff.

"I'm sorry, Dr. Villare has had a long night, and he came home to get some rest only a few hours ago."

Dr. Villare. How strange to hear the housekeeper use the name Jeff associated with his father to refer to him. Others had called him that, and it seemed natural, but to hear Mrs. Mike say it sounded out of place.

And to whom was she speaking? Did Doc Broussard need his services again?

As much as he'd like to hide, to ignore the call to work once more, he knew he could not. He'd promised he would remain available as long as he was needed.

"Mrs. Mike?" Jeff stepped into the hall and froze when he saw Angeline Breaux standing at the open front door.

He went forward and took his friend by the hand. "Angeline, come in." To his surprise, she stood firm.

"No, thank you." She winced as she slipped her hand from his. "Actually, Mama sent me to fetch you to see to Amalie."

The mention of the young girl's name brought back an image of her wan appearance two nights ago. "What's happened?"

"Could I tell you on the way?" She curled her fingers into fists and hid her hands behind her back. "Mama's powerful worried, and I'd hate to keep her waiting."

"What's wrong?"

"I told you, Mama thinks Amalie's fever is a bad sign. She wants you to come see."

He moved a bit closer. "No, I mean what's wrong with you?"

Before she could answer, he reached for her arms and turned her small hands up so he could examine them. Both palms were raw with abrasions, and a blister ran across the length of her right thumb.

He turned to the housekeeper. "Mrs. Mike, fetch my bag, would you? It's in Pop's office, on the desk, I believe." As she scurried past, he returned his attention to Angeline. "How did this happen?"

"Really, Jefferson, *sa fait pas rien.*"

"Yes, it matters."

He acknowledged the housekeeper's return by motioning for her to follow him into the kitchen. With difficulty, he managed to get Angeline inside the house and settled in a chair at the kitchen table.

While he bound her wounds, she told him the story of her arrival at his doorstep. "You rowed all this way, *Ma Chere?*"

When she nodded, he replied, "Well if you have no objections, we'll leave your old pirogue here and take Pop's Model A. I'll have someone bring it back before nightfall. I promise."

"A motorcar?" She looked away. "Oh, I don't know."

Jeff smiled. For the bayou people, getting around by boat had been a tradition carried down through the centuries. Bad roads and wet conditions made driving treacherous in wet weather and merely bumpy and inconvenient in dry weather. Only in rare instances was it their first choice of transportation.

"Angeline, have you ever ridden in a motorcar?"

"Once," she said softly. "When I was a little girl, Papa's uncle came to visit, and he took us for a ride."

"Oh? Did you enjoy it?"

She nodded. "Very much, at least until that motorcar hit a slick spot and nearly slid into the bayou."

"That must have been quite a ride." He grasped her elbow and turned her toward the door. "I promise I will stay out of the bayou on this trip." He paused to glance over his shoulder. "Mrs. Mike, would you bring my bag out to the car?"

After helping Angeline into the Model A, he slid behind the steering wheel and placed the bag between them. To her credit, Angeline said nothing as he pulled out of the driveway and into the sparse traffic on Jackson Street. She merely held on to the edge of the seat and sat ramrod straight, her eyes barely blinking.

"Are you all right?" he finally asked.

She nodded, a stiff nod that did nothing to convince him of the earnestness of her answer. He searched his mind for something, anything, that might cause her to feel at ease, but nothing came to mind. Of course, a few stray memories of times they'd shared did occur to him, but he doubted the wisdom of mentioning them. With his train tickets bought, the last thing he needed was to schedule another trip—this one down memory lane. After the fiasco at the Breaux house two nights ago, he'd learned his lesson.

No, this visit to check on her sister would be all business, no social call. As soon as he administered treatment to Amalie, he would be on his way, never to return to Bayou Nouvelle and Angeline Breaux.

It was the only way, really.

As they rolled along the streets of Latanier, he noticed Angeline relax a bit. She'd released her death grip on the edge of the seat and appeared to be sitting comfortably with her hands grasped in her lap. Only the white of her knuckles gave away the depth of her fear.

"So, Angeline, tell me what's ailing your sister."

She sighed. "At first we thought it might be a touch of the croup or maybe something she ate. She was a little feverish and just didn't act like herself."

"What sort of treatment did she receive?"

"Mama put a poultice on her and I kept a cool cloth on her head." She paused. "I knew she didn't feel good for sure when she just lay there and let us mess with her. That little Amalie, she's not one to sit still."

Jeff slowed to allow a horse and buggy to cross First Avenue. "How long ago did she first exhibit these new symptoms?"

"About three days ago, maybe four."

"I remember she slept through the evening I spent out at your place. Has she been sleeping excessively?"

"She does seem to be tired a lot of the time."

"And Mathilde, has she had any more fainting episodes?"

Angeline nodded. "Just this morning she nearly dropped one of Mama's good teacups on the floor when she about passed out. If she had other fits like that, she hasn't said."

"Is there anything else you can tell me about Amalie's condition and Mathilde's?"

Only when she'd said her last words on the subject did he allow his mind to wander past the confines of the motorcar to what might lie ahead of them. Dare he consider little Amalie, and perhaps even Mathilde, might bear the signs of influenza? If so, the rest of the Breaux family would be in danger of contracting the deadly disease.

"Do you think you can fix my Amalie?"

"I think God can fix anything, Angeline. Whether He uses me to do it is another matter entirely." He met her gaze and attempted a smile. "I will do my best though."

And I'll pray my best is good enough.

Jeff turned the car off the main road and onto the narrow lane leading toward the Breaux home. Whatever he found there, God would go before him.

"Oh, and Jefferson, I've been meaning to thank you for what you did for me the night you shared gumbo with us." She offered him a radiant smile. "Papa never knew his pants went to town and back."

They shared a laugh, and Jeff felt a perplexing stab of pain. How wonderful it would be to laugh with her more often.

Moments into the drive down the ancient thoroughfare, the road fell into shadows as the trees hung low and thick. Birds dipped and flew, teasing the old car as it lumbered past. In a matter of minutes, time had rolled backward, and except for the modern motorcar, he could have been traveling a road that looked the same a century ago.

"Jefferson, do you ever wonder why God put all of us on earth to be so different?"

Surprised, he swung his gaze to meet Angeline's stare. "Now that's an interesting thought. What do you mean?"

"Well, look at us." She smiled a wry smile. "If ever two people were more different from the beginning, I can't imagine it. I mean, you're a big city doctor and I'm just a simple bayou girl."

Jeff shook his head. "Angeline Breaux, there is nothing simple about you."

"But don't you see? There's nothing wrong with being simple, Jefferson. In fact, I rather prefer it. It's you I'm concerned for."

"How so?" he asked as the car lurched over ruts in the little road.

Angeline grabbed for the door handle to keep from sliding forward. Her face told him she bore the bouncing about much better than she had the miles they'd driven in the city. Perhaps the nearness to home helped.

"Well, I just can't imagine being up North among strangers who talk funny and move so fast. I saw downtown New York on the news reels at the picture show once, and it looked like there were more people on that one sidewalk than we have in the whole state of Louisiana."

A pair of dogs lounged in the road, and Jeff honked the horn to scatter them into the thicket. "I hardly think New York's that big."

"It's bigger than Latanier, and that's all I need to know." She released her grip on the door as the Model A rolled over a smoother patch of road. "I don't know why anyone would want to leave such a beautiful place."

Why indeed? And yet the beauty of the lush green landscape and the brilliant blue sky paled in comparison to the dark-haired Acadian beauty seated beside him.

For a moment, he allowed himself the luxury of imagining a life spent in the bayou country. With the exception of times like now, when mysterious fevers swept the area, his would be a life of simplicity.

He remembered the kiss he shared with Angeline and touched his finger to his lips. If only he could give up the life he felt called toward in order to have more of those kisses, perhaps a lifetime of them.

Unfortunately, he had a one-way train ticket to New York dated for two days hence. Come Wednesday morning, he would leave the bayou and Angeline behind.

Or would he?

Lord, is that why You kept her in my mind all these years? Could I have misunderstood Your direction for my life? Do You want me to pursue a relationship with Angeline Breaux?

twelve

What a strange expression Jefferson wore! Had she said something wrong? Of course, he was leaving in two days, so maybe he didn't like what she said about staying here.

For the next few minutes, they rode along in silence. Angeline couldn't think of anything else to say, and Jefferson obviously didn't want to make conversation either. She settled for worrying with the bandages on her hands until Jefferson finally told her to leave them alone.

Mama met them in the yard as the motorcar pulled alongside the house. Several of the little ones tagged behind her, but when the vehicle roared to a stop, they scattered to the porch.

"Thank the Lord you're here, Jefferson. My Amalie, she's sick, and my Mathilde, she's not looking so well either, no."

Jefferson grabbed his medical bag and climbed out of the motorcar. Angeline tried several times to open the door but failed. Thankfully, Jefferson noticed her troubles and circled around to help her out.

"Thank you," she said softly as she climbed out on shaking legs. The trip might have been faster than a pirogue ride, but it certainly wasn't the way she intended to go again.

"Where are they?" he asked.

"Follow me, *Bebe*. I put them both in the back bedroom away from the rest of the babies."

"That's a good idea," Jefferson said. "Keep them separated from everyone else. I don't want to think this could be contagious, but there's no need in subjecting the children to harm."

"Yes, that's what I thought too. I don't want to take no chances. I made plans to send the children, all but the littlest one, to Tante Flo's for today. Flo, she don't got no little ones over there, and they always like to spend the night."

"That's good," Jefferson said. "It sounds like they will be well taken care of. Depending on what my diagnosis is, they may have to stay a few days. Will that be a problem?"

Worry creased Mama's brow, but she put on a smile. "No, of course not. Flo, she would keep them forever and a day if I let her."

"Well, I don't think it will take that long for the girls to recover. Now, why don't you show me where they are so I can take a look and see what we're dealing with?"

"Of course, Jefferson. Follow me, eh?"

He stepped through the front door and followed Mama through the main room of the house and into the little bedroom at the back. Through the door, she could see Mathilde sleeping soundly on one big bed, while Amalie lay wide-eyed and propped up on a mountain of pillows on the other.

Before entering the room, Jefferson put down his medical bag and held up his hand to stop Mama. "I can't let you go in there, Mrs. Breaux." His gaze rested on the bulge at her waist. "In your delicate condition, it wouldn't be safe, at least not if it's what I fear it might be."

"I hadn't thought of that." Mama rested a hand on her stomach and turned to Angeline. "You go help Jefferson, you hear? I'll wait right here outside the door, but you call me if you need something, eh?"

"We will, Mama." Angeline stood at the side of the bed and watched Jefferson bend down to sit next to Amalie. "What do you want me to do, Jefferson?"

"Hand me my bag, please." When Angeline complied, Jefferson reached for it, then turned his attention to Amalie. "Your sister says you're not feeling well. Is that the truth or did she just come all the way to Latanier to get me so we could have some more of that good gumbo she makes?"

"I like her gumbo too," Amalie said with a weak smile, "but today my tummy's not feeling good."

Jefferson cast a quick glance over his shoulder at Angeline and grinned. "It's not? Well, let's see if I can fix that. Is there anything else I need to examine while I'm looking at your tummy? Maybe you need your chin hairs checked."

Amalie's smile brightened, and her fingers reached from beneath the blanket to cradle her chin. "I don't got no chin hairs. See?"

"You don't?" Jefferson reached inside his medical bag and pulled out a small instrument. "Well, let me make sure they're not growing on the inside." He placed his hand over hers and gently opened her mouth to peer inside. "You're right. There's none in here."

"I told you so." She pulled the covers up to her nose and looked up at Angeline. "He's a funny man. Are you sure he's a doctor?"

Angeline nodded. "Yes, I'm sure. Now behave and let him work."

Jefferson slipped the instrument back in the bag. "Now let's see. What else do I have in here?"

He made a big show of fishing around in the bag while Amalie slowly let go of the covers. When the little girl leaned over the side of the bed to peer into the bag, Jefferson pulled out a stethoscope and said, "Aha! Look what I've found."

Amalie's squeal of glee awoke Mathilde. "What is he doing here?" she whispered.

Angeline sat on the edge of Mathilde's bed and placed her palm on her sister's damp brow. It felt warm but not exceptionally so. "Hush, Matty. Jefferson's here to doctor the both of you. He's looking at Amalie first, then he'll look at you."

Mathilde nodded and closed her eyes. "All right," she said with what sounded like the last of her breath.

Jefferson listened to Amalie's chest, looked into her ears, and completed his examination by taking her pulse. All the while, the little girl's brown eyes watched him intently. When he'd tucked her back under the covers, he pulled out a small notebook and began to scribble.

From the door, Mama called to Jefferson. "What you find wrong with my Amalie?"

"Mama, you're not supposed to be in here," Angeline said.

She feigned innocence. "I'm not in there. I'm out here."

"Mama!"

Jefferson looked up sharply. "Please, Mrs. Breaux. You cannot allow yourself to get sick, not with other children to tend and a baby on the way."

Mama's expression turned grave. "So you think it might be. . ."

Influenza. Angeline knew Mama couldn't say the word.

"I'd rather we spoke privately after I examine Mathilde."

Angeline knew for sure that her sister was sick when she allowed the doctor to complete his exam without so much as batting an eye. For Mathilde Breaux to miss a chance at flirting, she had to be ill.

Once more, Jefferson wrote in his notebook, then folded it into his medical bag along with his supplies.

"Why don't we let these ladies get some rest?"

"Angie, will you come back and tell me a story?" Amalie asked with a yawn.

"Of course, Sweetheart." Angeline straightened the little girl's covers and pushed an errant curl off her forehead. "You just close your eyes and start thinking about which one you want to hear. I'll be back as soon as I can."

Amalie nodded, snuggling deeper into the mound of pillows. Odds were, by the time Angeline returned, her sister would be sound asleep. A quick check of Mathilde told her she would also sleep soundly.

Angeline and Mama followed Jefferson back outside onto

the front porch. Mama sank onto the bench by the door and rested her hands on her knees.

"So what is it, Jefferson? What's wrong with my girls, eh?"

Jefferson's gaze went from Angeline to Mama and back to Angeline. "I'm encouraged that neither girl is exhibiting all the symptoms of influenza, but I'm troubled that they do have the fever and aches. Have you noticed any coughing?"

Mama shook her head and looked to Angeline. "No," Angeline said, "I don't think so. Mathilde's fainted a few times, and Amalie does nothing but sleep."

He looked relieved. "Good. That just might mean these two will get well on their own."

"Back in 1918 when the influenza hit us so hard here, we used to give the sick ones a drink of sugar water with kerosene. It seemed to help." Mama looked up at Jefferson. "What do you think, eh?"

"I think that probably isn't necessary, Mrs. Breaux. At this point bed rest is what's going to make them better." He focused his attention on Angeline. "I'll need you to monitor the girls for signs of complications and see to their needs. Your mother or any of your siblings are not to go near them, do you understand?"

Angeline nodded.

"Mrs. Breaux, I cannot overstate the importance of isolating Mathilde and Amalie until their symptoms subside. If this is influenza—and we pray it isn't—they will pass it on to anyone else in close contact within a matter of days."

"Oh, I don't want that."

"No," he said, "you don't." Again, he addressed Angeline. "They will need a typical invalid diet—broth, liquids, and the like. Can you handle that?"

"Of course."

"And if either of them develops a cough, a headache, or any other symptom that worries you, fetch me immediately." His mouth quirked into a smile. "And promise me you won't come by pirogue unless you remember to put on some gloves."

Angeline looked down at her bandaged palms and matched his smile. "I promise."

"Fine then." He reached to take Mama's hand and shake it. "I want you to concern yourself with seeing to the needs of your healthy children and let Angeline tend to the sick ones. Will you promise me that?"

Mama seemed to contemplate the question a moment, and Angeline wondered if she might not agree. After all, Mama generally took charge of everything and everyone in the Breaux household. Delegating anything of importance didn't come easily to her.

Even as she spoke, she looked undecided. "I will do that, Jefferson, but only because I know you're a smart man, and you know what's best for the *bebes*."

He shouldered his bag. "I appreciate that, Mrs. Breaux. Knowing I will only have two Breaux girls to doctor eases my mind greatly."

Jefferson reached for Angeline's hand. "Walk with me to the car, would you?"

Their gazes collided. Somehow Angeline managed to nod and follow him down the porch steps.

"So you'll be taking care of my girls yourself, then?" Mama called.

When Jefferson smiled, Angeline's heart melted. "Yes, Ma'am, I will."

Angeline chose her words carefully. "But I thought you were leaving on Wednesday."

His smile chased away all her worries. "So did I. I guess God had other plans," he said as he gave her a quick kiss on the cheek and made his exit.

As she watched the motorcar disappear around the bend in the road, Angeline's heart soared, then sank. Jefferson was staying. This had been her dream once, to have Jefferson Villare back in the bayou country and back in her life. Now that God had brought it within her grasp, it seemed He—or at least Papa—might be taking it away.

"Who was that who done drove off from here?"

Angeline whirled around. "Papa! I thought you and Ernest were gone for the whole day."

"Well, I'm not. I sent your brother off to finish checking the trot lines while I came home to see about my girls."

"They're sleeping. Amalie seems a bit better this afternoon, but all Mathilde wants to do is sleep." She shrugged. "It sure makes for a quiet house when those two aren't up and causing excitement."

Papa nodded. "I can just imagine. Now who was that in the motorcar?"

Leave it to Papa not to let loose of a question once he'd asked it. If she didn't tell him, Mama would. Better she do it.

Debating the amount of information she gave Papa didn't take long. There was no use aggravating him more than necessary.

"The doctor. He came to examine the girls."

There, the truth had been told. If Papa asked, she would tell him the rest. Jefferson Villare *was* a doctor, after all.

Her father gave her a sideways glance, then linked arms with her. "And what did he say? How's my Amalie and Mathilde?"

"The girls are resting," she said. "The doctor says that's best."

Papa's face turned grave. "Does he think it might be the influenza?"

"He's not sure," she replied. "We're to keep them away from the others and especially away from Mama."

He chuckled and turned her toward the house. Angeline fell in step alongside him.

"Now that's going to be a trick in itself. My Clothilde, she don't like to be told not to mess with her babies, especially when they're sick." He nudged her shoulder with his. "And my Angie, she's the same way as her mama, eh?"

"About some things, I suppose," she admitted with a grin.

"Some things like doing the right thing when her papa and mama tell her to?"

Angeline stopped in her tracks. "What are you talking about, Papa? When haven't I done the right thing?"

"Theophile Breaux, what are you doing home in the middle of the afternoon, eh?"

"You sound just like your daughter, Cleo." He turned his attention to Angeline. "I've got some good news for you, Angie, and I can't wait to tell you and your mama both."

She tried not to cringe. Papa's good news might be just that—good news—or it might be something else entirely.

"This would happen to be about Nicolas Arceneaux, would it?"

Papa smiled and patted her head. "Now don't you worry your pretty self about Monsieur Arceneaux just yet. I got it all worked out, and you're gonna be so happy."

"Happy?" Her feelings went toward the opposite emotion.

"Yes, Girlie, now let's go where your mama can hear." He led her toward the porch steps. "No sense in me telling this story twice."

"Papa, please tell me you didn't go and make any promises to Nicolas. I never did answer him when he proposed, you know."

Dread turned to something worse when she saw her papa's smile fade. "It don't make no never mind whether you said yes yet. Nicolas and me, we know you're gonna be happy with him, and that's what counts, isn't it?"

"What counts is what God wants, Papa."

"I know that," Papa said as he looked past her rather than at her. A sadness washed over his tanned features. "And God, He don't break up families, no. He keeps us together for always."

"But, Papa, are you sure God wants me married off to Nicolas Arceneaux?" When he didn't answer immediately, she added, "Or is that just what you want so I can be assured of not leaving the bayou?"

Papa's startled look gave her reason to hope he might actually be considering her question. She said a little prayer that the Lord would soften his heart and make him see what was so obvious to her. Nicolas Arceneaux was not the husband for her.

"What're you talking about, eh?" Mama called. "I see you two are conspiring."

"Well, now, I'm glad you asked, Clothilde." He crossed the porch to greet Mama with a kiss. "I was just telling Angie that I had good news for the whole family. Now let me go see to my two sick ones, then I'll tell you all about it."

"But, Theo, Ernest isn't here," Mama said. "If it's that important, shouldn't we wait on him?"

Papa waved off Mama's question with a shake of his head and disappeared into the house. "He'll be here soon enough," came the answer through the open door.

Angeline settled next to Mama on the bench. "What do you think Papa's up to this time, Mama?"

Her mother shook her head. "I don't know, *Bebe*, but I think it might have something to do with that man there."

Mama pointed toward the west, where Ernest was walking toward them across the lawn. At his side were Nicolas Arceneaux and a gray-haired man in a dark suit.

As they neared the house, she realized the identity of the elderly man. It was the local preacher, Reverend Dautrive.

thirteen

Jefferson lay atop the sheets and stared at the ceiling in his childhood room. A painting of the constellations fanned out from the four corners of the light fixture, a fanciful feature courtesy of his mother.

She'd been the artist in the family, a woman with a creative flair and a bent for the whimsical. Losing her had meant losing nearly everything.

Everything except Pop and his best friend, Angeline.

Now Pop was gone to spend eternity with Mom. That left only Angeline.

He rolled to his side and stared at the train ticket on the nightstand. Torn in half, part of it lay atop a stack of his favorite books, while the rest sat teetering on the edge. Blowing a hard breath sent the ticket flying, and he watched it sail across the beams of light filtering through the shutters on the western-facing side of the house. It landed at the feet of his old rocking horse, a relic of a childhood he barely remembered.

"Tomorrow I'll have to let the landlady know I won't be arriving as planned," he said to the old horse. "Wonder what she'll make of that."

He shifted back into his original position, cradling his hands behind his head. "I wonder what I should make of that, Lord."

Why do you have to make anything of it? Stop trying to figure everything out and rest in Me.

"Rest?" Jeff let out a strained chuckle. "Who could ever get any rest here?"

You could, if you would stop trying so hard.

Outside, the strains of the evening were coming alive, a familiar combination of crickets, night birds, and the occasional barking dog. Soon the sun would set, and the night would settle around the old house.

Mrs. Mike had left enough food for four grown men wrapped up in the kitchen, and he'd promised her he would try and eat something before bed. In a few minutes, after a bit more rest, he would get up, go downstairs, and make an attempt.

But for now, moving seemed out of the question. His old bed, with the feather mattress that seemed to mold to his form, refused to let him go.

He gave in to its embrace and thought once more of how it felt to spend time with Angeline Breaux. Yes, those moments were every bit as comfortable as this feather bed, this familiar room, this old house. Perhaps that's why he'd chosen to delay his departure.

Jeff allowed himself to believe that, all the time knowing if he dared, he would realize a deeper, more permanent reason for spending time with Angeline. Unfortunately, the Lord hadn't yet told him how he could have the one he'd always loved and the career he was called to. Until He did, Jeff was stuck waiting.

"Excuse me," he said to the ceiling. "I'm not waiting, I'm *resting*."

No, you're not, but you could be. Stop trying to control things and turn it over to Me. You can have all that you want and more, but you've got to stop trying to make things happen by planning your whole life at once.

"But, Lord, You say in Your Word that we fail for lack of planning. What about that?"

I also say that a man plans his steps, but the Lord knows the direction he will go.

"All right, Lord. You win."

I always do, My Son. Now rest.

With a sigh, Jeff closed his eyes and, for the first time in days, slept soundly, even though it was hours before bedtime.

æ

Mama put a hand on Angeline's shoulder. "Angeline, go on in the house and see to your sisters. Let me handle the menfolk, eh?" She rose and waved toward the trio now crossing the lawn. "And tell your papa I'd like to have a word with him, would you?"

"Of course, Mama," she said as she walked inside. She met Papa and conveyed the message, scooting out of his way before he could ask any more questions.

She stepped into the bedroom and closed the door partway behind her. If anyone went looking for her, they would have to come into the room to find her, but if anything interesting was said—or if anyone called her name—she would hear.

Both her sisters slept soundly, leaving Angeline with nothing to do but tidy up the small space. Exhausting all the possibilities for cleaning within minutes, Angeline sat on the edge of Amalie's bed and began to pray as she stroked the little girl's dark curls.

Father, You are in control, and I know that. Heal these sisters of mine, and keep whatever is ailing them from spreading to the others, especially to Mama, who needs to take care of herself and the baby coming in a few months.

As to the situation going on outside right now, I ask that You step in and do something to show what You want done. Keep Papa mindful of the fact that You have the last say on everything, and please, let Your will—not Papa's will—be done in the matter of choosing a husband for me.

She almost added something about Jefferson but thought better of it. If the Creator of the universe didn't know what was best for her, no one did.

Still, she hoped He wouldn't make the same choice Papa had made for her.

"I've made my choice and that's that." Papa's voice echoed in the small room, causing Amalie to stir.

"Angie, what's wrong?" she murmured.

"Hush now, Little Sister," Angeline said as she smoothed Amalie's damp brow. "That's just Papa, and he's all fired up about something."

About me, I'm sure.

"Angie?" This time Mathilde spoke. "Is that handsome fisherman here again?"

Angeline looked up, startled. "Yes, actually he is, along with the preacher."

Mathilde smiled. "He's quite handsome."

"You mentioned that, Matty," she said as she rose and reached to straighten the bedcovers Mathilde had tangled. "Now get some sleep."

"I will," she whispered. "Maybe I'll dream about fishing. Or maybe I'll just dream about stealing your Nicolas for myself."

"Now, that's one dream I would share with you."

Angeline chuckled. Even in the middle of her illness, Mathilde was thinking of men. Poor foolish girl with her silly imaginings. She wouldn't be so fast to fall in love if she knew what a mess of trouble it could bring.

Actually, Papa's threat of sending her to the nunnery was starting to look better than the alternative. Even if Jefferson was interested in something more than a fleeting romance, and there was no evidence he was, she would have to defy Papa and leave Mama, the babies, and the bayou to follow him. Could she do that?

"I just don't know," she said softly.

The alternative was to be the dutiful daughter and follow her papa's wishes to marry Nicolas Arceneaux. She would stay among family, for sure, and Mama would never want for her help.

"But I don't love him."

"I know you don't, *Bebe*. That's why you're going to do just what I say."

Angeline jumped and whirled around to stare at the doorway. Mama stood just outside the room.

"How are my girls?" she asked as she peered around the doorframe for a better look at Mathilde and Amalie.

"Resting comfortably," Angeline said. "Matty feels a little warm, but Amalie seems to be doing well. I don't think either of them is hungry, but Jefferson says they need to keep up their strength. At least both are drinking their water." She picked up the two empty water glasses from the nightstand and walked toward the door. "Maybe I ought to fix them bowls of chicken broth. We still have some of that chicken stock left over, don't we? I could go do that right now."

"Angie, you're a natural born nurse if I ever did see one," Mama said.

"Well, I don't know about that," Angeline replied as she left the room and closed the door behind her. "Now what did you mean when you first came to the door? You said something about my doing exactly what you said."

Mama placed her finger to her lips to silence Angeline. Motioning to the back door, she turned and headed that way. Angeline followed, still holding the water glasses.

"Go put those in the summer kitchen and wash your hands. I'll wait right here," Mama said as she stood on the back steps.

When Angeline returned, the faint sound of male voices told her that the men were still there.

"Mama, what is Papa doing with Nicolas and the pastor?"

Rather than answer, Mama headed down the narrow path that led through the thicket and ended at the banks of the Bayou Nouvelle. With every step, Angeline's worries increased. The combination of Nicolas, Papa, and Reverend Dautrive could only mean one thing.

A wedding was afoot.

Her wedding.

Keeping silent was nearly impossible, so she shouted her thoughts to the Lord in prayer. *Please hear me, Father! Please don't let them do this to me. I don't love this man.*

A quietness settled in her heart as she heard the gentle response. *I know, My child. But now you must wait on Me.*

Angeline halted her pace to stare up into the canopy of trees and the blue sky beyond. A single cloud, wispy like pulled cotton, teased the edges of the trees and floated slowly on the breeze.

"Then do something," she whispered.

Mama cast a glance over her shoulder. "What's that, *Bebe*? Something wrong, and you can't walk no more?"

"No, Mama," she answered as she fell back into step behind her mother. "I can walk just fine."

It's the waiting I'm having trouble with.

Finally Mama stopped at the edge of the bayou and settled down on a grassy spot in the shade. "Sit here, *Bebe*," she said as she patted the place next to her. "You and me, we got some talking to do."

Dread formed in her chest, and she knew the thing she feared most would soon happen. Strange, but she knew. "It's about Papa and Nicolas, isn't it?"

Mama nodded. "The wedding, they've started planning it."

Everything inside her crumpled. Where was God? How could He allow this to happen? Couldn't He see she did not love Nicolas Arceneaux?

"Oh, Mama, how can I stop this?" she cried. "I just can't marry Nicolas. I can't. I don't love him. I'll *never* love him."

"Hush, now, Angeline. This crying and worrying won't change a thing. You know you can't stop this and neither can I." She lifted Angeline's chin and looked into her eyes. "But God can."

"Yes, Mama, He can." She swiped the back of her hand across her eyes to push away the tears. "But will He?"

Mama leaned back and looked up into the sky. "I pray He will, *Bebe*. But until He does, you and me, we've got to do some things."

Angeline sniffed. "What kind of things?"

"Now I want you to listen to everything I've got to say before you talk, you hear?"

"Yes, Mama."

"All right, the first thing you and me have to do is start planning this wedding of yours." She held up a hand to stop Angeline's protest. "Now I know what you're gonna say. You don't want no wedding, eh?"

"That's right."

"Well, just because you don't want a wedding, that doesn't mean there won't be one. Do you understand?" When Angeline nodded, Mama continued. "We can go about this thing in two ways. The first way is to do what you're doing right now."

"What do you mean?"

"I mean, you can go kicking and screaming all the way to the altar with your papa following right behind you holding his big old shotgun and the whole town watching. Is that what you want, eh?"

An image rose in her mind. She could see the interior of the little church where the Breaux family had worshiped for three generations. In every row of seats were friends, family members, and townspeople, all dressed in their Sunday best to attend a wedding.

White bunting had been tied to the ends of the old cypress pews, and big white ribbons decorated the edges of the pastor's lectern. Her groom, dressed in a suit of dark color, awaited her arrival with his head bowed, as did Reverend Dautrive.

Such a beautiful picture it was, and then she and Papa emerged from the back of the church, and a gasp went up from the crowd. At her side, Papa stood. At his side stood the big shotgun.

The crowd began to laugh. Worse, so did the pastor and her groom.

Angeline dissolved the image with a shake of her head. "Oh, Mama, that would be awful."

"It would indeed." She offered a wry smile and batted at a mosquito buzzing around her bare arm. "Now, if you'll listen to your mama, there just might be a better way of going about this."

Hope dawned inside Angeline, and she sent it skyward with another prayer. Her mother was wise, especially in the way of love and marriage. Surely she could give her some way out of this mess.

"What do you have in mind, Mama?"

"Well, what I have in mind is this." She grinned and clapped her hands together in excitement. "You and me, we're gonna plan a wedding, eh?"

fourteen

Again Mama stopped Angeline's protest with a wave of her hand. "Now just let me finish. You were always an impatient child, Angeline. Why don't you sit on your questions and give me a minute to explain?"

"I'm sorry."

She took a deep breath and let it out slowly. "God and me, we've been talking a whole bunch about this problem of yours, and I think He wants us to just go on about our business and plan you a pretty wedding."

Angeline's heart sank. "Forgive me, Mama, but I don't see how giving in to Papa's demands and planning a wedding for Nicolas and me is going to get me out of this mess."

"First off, let's get this straight, Young Lady. Your papa is the head of this household, and as such, what he says goes, you hear?" When Angeline nodded, Mama continued. "So now that we got that straight, we know we can't just tell him you're not gonna marry the Arceneaux boy. That would be disobedient to Papa and to God, since He sent Papa to be in authority over you long as you live in our house, eh? Tell me you understand that much."

Why did Mama have to make so much sense? It would be so easy to protest the unfairness of the situation by refusing to cooperate. And with Jefferson Villare's kisses still warm on her lips, even after all this time, she desperately wanted to protest a marriage to someone else.

"I understand."

"Well, all right then. You asked me how this is going to help. Angie, *Bebe,* I don't know, but I trust that *Le Bon Dieu,*

He does. My prayers, they tell me I need to help plan a wedding for my Angeline, and that's what I'm gonna do. I don't know how God's gonna fix this, but I do know He will. Do you trust Him?"

Did she? How easy it was to claim trust in the Lord when things were going well! How much more difficult to profess that same trust when God seemed to be doing the exact opposite of what made sense.

"Yes, Mama, I trust Him," she said finally.

"Good," Mama said. "Then let's go visit with the menfolk. I'm sure they're wondering where we got off to."

Angeline stood and helped her mother to her feet. "You're not going to be able to do that much longer," she said.

"I know that, *Bebe.*" Mama rubbed her back, then dusted off her skirt. All at once, her face turned serious. "Before we go back and talk to the menfolk, I need to ask you something, and I want you to tell me the honest truth. Will you do that?"

Dread returned, and Angeline swiped at the grass on her legs rather than look directly at her mother. "Of course I will. I'm always honest with you, Mama."

"Good." She paused. "I want to know *why* you don't want to marry Nicolas Arceneaux."

Angeline swung her gaze to meet her mother's. "Well, to start off, I don't even know the man. He seems nice enough and all, but I can't imagine spending the rest of my life with a stranger."

"Fair enough." Mama seemed to consider the statement for a moment. "Any other reasons? I mean, he's handsome enough, and he does come from a good family."

"Yes, that's true," she said. "But I don't care about those things."

"All right then, let me see. He's a hard-working man, that's for sure, eh? While he was here, he helped your papa and Ernest every day and worked as hard as two men. You can't fault him for being lazy, no, not at all."

"No, I don't suppose you could fault him for that." Again Angeline looked away.

"And he loves the Lord; you know that."

"Yes, I believe he does."

Mama placed a hand on Angeline's shoulder and sighed. "Then why don't you just come out and tell your mama why you don't want to marry a handsome, hard-working young man from a good family, eh?"

The truth lay just beyond her ability to speak it. Even to try would be silly. No two people were more unevenly matched than she and Jefferson Villare. How could a simple bayou girl ever have designs on a rich, city-bound doctor?

"I can't, Mama."

"I believe you can," she said softly. "You might as well tell me. The Lord already knows."

Angeline took a deep breath and let it out slowly. Mama was right. The Lord did already know. The truth be told, Mama probably knew as well.

"I can't marry Nicolas Arceneaux because I've been in love with Jefferson Villare as long as I can remember. I'd rather spend my life as an old maid helping you than to spend it married to someone other than Jefferson."

There, she'd said it. Angeline closed her eyes and waited for the lecture she knew her mother would deliver. Instead, she got only silence. When she opened her eyes, she saw that Mama had already begun to walk toward the house.

Mustering up as much dignity as she could manage, she followed Mama back down the path and out into the clearing. As they neared the house, Angeline could hear the raised voices of the men along with their laughter.

When Mama stopped abruptly, Angeline almost ran into her. "Angie," she said softly, "guard your heart. As a woman, I understand how you feel, eh? But as your mother, I have to remind you that you've got to be obedient to the Lord, even if He says you must give up this man you love."

Angeline nodded. "I will."

"It's gonna hurt if it happens this way, but you'll just have to trust that *Le Bon Dieu*, He don't make no mistakes." She smiled. "His is the better way, even if we don't always agree."

"I know," Angeline said.

"Good." Her mother seemed to study her a moment. "Now put on your prettiest smile, and let's go talk about a wedding that might or might not happen, eh?"

They crossed the distance to the house arm in arm, each matching the pace of the other. With every step, Angeline begged the Lord to give her the strength to put her own wishes aside and follow His. By the time she reached the back steps, she almost felt like she could accomplish this.

Inside the house, Angeline said one last prayer. *Lord, You know my faults. Please let me do this through Your strength and not try it through mine.*

"Clothilde, where you at, Sweetie?" Papa called. "Come bring yourself out here and fetch Angeline with you."

"Right here, Theo." Mama emerged from the bedroom to run her fingers through her hair and check her smile in the pier glass. "Now remember what I said, Angie. You be obedient even if you don't *feel* like it, you hear?"

"Yes, Mama." Angeline followed her through the house and out onto the front porch.

When she appeared, all conversation ceased. Nicolas, who stood apart from the two older men, gazed at her with interest while Papa and the reverend looked as if they'd been caught conspiring.

"Come on over here, Angie girl," Papa said.

She stepped around Mama to stand at Papa's side. He gave her a hug, then held her at arm's length. "You look mighty pretty this afternoon."

"Miss Angeline, you do look like a breath of fresh air." Reverend Dautrive removed his straw hat and mopped at his bald head with a white handkerchief. "I wonder if we will have the pleasure of hearing you sing again this Sunday."

"I don't know yet, Reverend," she said. "I suppose I'll find out tomorrow at choir practice."

"My girl, she can sing, that's for sure," Papa said. "Oh, you should hear her. I'll tell you, it's like the angels done come to Bayou Nouvelle."

Mama merely nodded and settled on the little bench as if to watch the show. If only Angeline could join her and be a spectator, instead of the center of attention.

"Beauty and a voice to match."

The words came from behind her, where Nicolas Arceneaux stood leaning against the porch rail. When she turned, she saw him smile.

"That's right," Papa said. "And don't forget she can cook too." He turned his attention to Nicolas. "Did I tell you she's right handy with the cleaning and the little ones? Why, I'd have to say there's not a thing my Angeline can't do."

"Papa, please," Angeline whispered. "You're embarrassing me."

"Now, Theo," Mama said, "you make it sound like Angie's a prize horse. Why you want to go and talk like that and make our girl feel all uncomfortable like, eh?"

An awkward silence enveloped the porch. Reverend Dautrive cleared his throat and pretended interest in a bee buzzing around Mama's Easter lilies while Papa simply glared at Mama. Nicolas Arceneaux, on the other hand, stared at Angeline openly. Finally, he squared his shoulders and crossed the porch to take her hand.

"I'm a plain-spoken man," he announced, "and I don't believe in a lot of fancy talk or beating around the bush. Why don't I just get to the heart of the matter for which we've all gathered?"

Angeline's gaze darted first to the left and then to the right, hoping for a distraction or possibly a place to run. She willed the baby to start crying, one of her sisters to call out for her, or even for the Lord to strike down a bolt of lightning that would call a halt to the whole proceedings.

Instead, a warm wind blew past, bringing the earthy scent of the bayou onto the porch. Somewhere to the east, a dog's bark chased the breeze.

"You go right on ahead, Young Man," Papa said.

Nicolas cleared his throat and stared into Angeline's eyes. "You and I have already talked about this. You know what I'm about to ask, don't you, Angeline?"

Tears welled up in Angeline's eyes. Somehow she managed to nod.

"And this time I'm going to stand right here and wait until I get an answer."

Dread closed around her throat. She couldn't have said a single word aloud at that moment if her life depended on it.

Please, Lord, please don't let him ask me to marry him.

"Angeline Breaux, it would be an honor for you to be my wife. Will you marry me?"

No, Father, don't make me answer him. Make this all go away.

Papa touched her shoulder and leaned toward her. The look in his eyes told her she could not stand mute forever. "Answer him, Angeline," he urged.

Reverend Dautrive slapped his straw hat back on his head and smiled as he stuffed his handkerchief into his pants pocket. "Oh, I do declare the tension is thick enough to cut with a knife. I'm probably speaking too soon, but the church calendar fills up fast in the summer. You'd need to get this wedding planned and done three weeks from Saturday, or you'll have to wait until September."

Angeline gulped. "Three weeks?"

"Now, Angie," Papa said. "You don't have nothing to wait

for, so why put off until the fall what we can get done in three weeks?" He turned to the reverend. "I say we take that spot on the calendar, eh?"

"Theo, hold up on yourself there," Mama called. "I think you'd better wait until the bride says yes before you book the wedding, eh?"

Nicolas lightly squeezed her hand and smiled. "Angeline?"

Do something, please, Lord.

An image of Jefferson crossed her mind and stuck there. He had stood on this very same porch only two nights ago and kissed her—twice. How could she agree to marry another when those kisses still lingered in her mind and heart? How could she say yes when her love belonged to another? How could she say no when Papa had all but sealed her fate well before now?

Your father wants the best for you, as do I.

"*Bebe,* does the cat got your tongue?" Mama asked. "It's not respectful to stand there like a statue. Better you say something before Mr. Arceneaux, he gets too old to take a bride."

God, if You're going to stop this, You need to act right now.

Angeline held her breath and waited for the answer she knew would come, the words that would end this. Instead, God was silent.

Her gaze landed on Nicolas Arceneaux and held there. "Yes, Nicolas," she whispered, "I will marry you."

Papa let out a whoop loud enough to be heard a mile down the road, while the Reverend Dautrive slapped Nicolas on the back and shook his hand. Mama, on the other hand, merely winked and disappeared into the house.

Angeline stood apart from the celebration and tried not to cry. Where was the Lord? Why hadn't He saved her?

Reverend Dautrive pulled a small notepad from his pocket and turned the pages. "As long as it's official, I might as well write the wedding down on the calendar." He made eye contact with Angeline. "We wouldn't want someone else to get that date, would we?"

"No," she whispered. "We wouldn't want that."

Only Nicolas seemed to detect the note of sadness that went along with her words. The look on his face told her as much.

"Now where did I put the calendar?" The reverend continued to flip the pages. "Well, here it is." Papa leaned toward him, as did Nicolas. "There, we have an opening in three weeks. I saw it just before I left the parsonage, and I believe it's on. . .uh oh."

"What?" Papa asked.

"Well. . ." The reverend removed his handkerchief to mop his brow, then took another look at the calendar.

"What is it, Reverend?" Nicolas chimed in.

Reverend Dautrive offered a weak smile and directed his gaze to Angeline. "Did I say three weeks? Well, that can't be right. It's not three weeks at all."

"Yes, you did," she said with a nod. *Oh, Lord, thank You for this delay,* she added silently.

"Just say it, Reverend," Papa said. "If it's not three weeks, then when's the big day?"

"Are we planning a wedding day?" Mama called from inside. "Wait just a minute and I'll be right there, eh?" She emerged onto the porch with the baby on her hip. "So what day are we gonna have this wedding, Reverend?"

The preacher smiled and held his notebook in the air. "According to this calendar here, there's just one day open this month. How's a week from Saturday?"

Angeline's jaw dropped as shock coursed through her. "But today's Monday." She fought to count the days. "That's less than two weeks away."

"Twelve days." Papa's grin widened. into a full-fledged smile.

Nicolas wrapped his arm around her waist and gathered

her to him. "Isn't that great, Angeline? Just twelve days and we'll be husband and wife."

She looked up into his eyes, and what she saw there surprised her. Nicolas didn't seem any more excited about the prospect of a wedding than she did.

fifteen

"So we've got twelve days to get to know one another," Nicolas said as they strolled down the banks of the Nouvelle. "That's not a long time, is it?"

Angeline batted at a strand of Spanish moss, then ducked to walk beneath it. "No, I suppose not."

You'll need to work fast, Lord.

"I don't suppose there's really much we have to know, is there, Angeline?" He paused. "The wedding will go on one way or another."

The truth in those words hit home, and Angeline had to blink back tears. "I suppose," she said as she turned away from his gaze to collect her thoughts.

They walked on, the sounds of the bayou filling the silence that fell between them. Occasionally, something would splash on the other bank, but nothing else disturbed the easy flow of the water.

"What's it like where you live, Nicolas?" she asked as she stepped around a hole in the path.

"Oh, I suppose it's much like this place, what with the bayou and all. Why?" He slowed his pace to reach for a stick and heave it toward the water.

"I don't know." She shrugged. "I suppose I was wondering what I would be facing when I left this place."

"You'll miss it, won't you?"

Angeline nodded. "Yes, but I can't stay. The house is overflowing now, and with another on the way, there's just not enough to go around. That's why Papa. . ."

"Bartered you off to a fisherman who lives just a little

way down the bayou?"

Stunned, she opened her mouth to speak and found the words were missing. She stared at him in horror.

"It's all right, *Ma Petite*," he whispered. "I don't mean to sound so harsh. After all, you and I, we were both bartered off, eh?"

"What do you mean?"

Nicolas stared past her with a faraway look in his eyes. "You might not believe this, but you're not the only one who doesn't particularly look forward to the wedding."

Something between surprise and relief seized her. "What do you mean?"

He returned his gaze to her and offered a weak smile. "I am ashamed to say that, although you are the prettiest flower that ever bloomed in this stretch of the bayou, you weren't my first choice as a bride."

"What?" His admission shocked her. At the same time, it made her feel a bit better about her feelings regarding Jefferson Villare. How could she hold this against Nicolas when she bore the same feelings in her heart? If God should choose to allow them to wed, He would enable them to handle this.

"You do not believe a man can reach my age and not lose his heart at least once, eh?"

So his was a love from the past. So much for feeling better about her current love for the young doctor.

"Whatever became of her?" Angeline asked.

"Ah, that is something I cannot think upon for it makes me sad."

The pain in his words made Angeline wince. "I'm sorry," she whispered.

"Me too," was his answer.

"Was she beautiful?" Why in the world did she ask that? Angeline looked at Nicolas and found him smiling. "Yes, every bit as beautiful as you. In fact, she is very much like you, only perhaps a bit more bossy." He shook his head. "But when I met her, I was not free to marry, so it wasn't to be, eh?"

"I suppose not."

Again, silence fell between them. This time Angeline used the opportunity to study her groom-to-be. Tall and strong, he wore the mantle of a son of the bayou with an easy grace.

He looked to be the type of man who would work hard, then come home to heft a baby or two atop his shoulders. Angeline prayed he was this kind of man, for she couldn't bear it if he were not.

"I have a big family, Angeline. I feel like I should warn you about that. Mama and Papa can't wait to meet you, and neither can my seven brothers and sisters. They'll all love you, I know, but when we get together, it can be loud. I'm the youngest of the bunch, so there are plenty of folks around the dinner table."

"Seven?" She laughed. "My goodness, that sounds like my family."

Nicolas stopped and turned to face her. "Actually, they are very much like your family, Angeline. Your people and our people, they settled the bayou and never forgot where they came from. Their blood, it lies beneath this land."

His fierceness startled her. "Yes," she whispered. "This is true."

"You don't speak the language of the Acadians much, do you, Angeline?"

"Oh, I don't know," she said as she averted her gaze. "I don't suppose we speak it as much as the older folks do, but we do mix the Acadian with the English. Why?"

"I just wondered. . ." He paused and seemed to be searching for the right words. "I wondered how you felt about your past, your history."

Angeline squared her shoulders. Where was this line of questioning going? Worse, what did he know about her past?

Surely someone hadn't told him about the gossip.

"I'm proud of my history. The Breaux family has lived on this bayou for two hundred years. There are more Breaux headstones in the church cemetery than anyone has time to count, and my mama's family has been here even longer." She paused to study his reaction. "I also have nothing to be ashamed of in my past."

A hawk swooped low and landed on the branch of a bald cypress nearby. Angeline watched the bird and wished she could fly away so easily.

Ah, but when you returned, your troubles would still be here, wouldn't they?

He barely blinked. "I didn't mean to say that you might be."

"Then what *did* you mean?"

"Angeline, I'm sorry. I'm not good at this thing of talking in circles, and that's what I've been doing." He took her hand in his. "I'm just going to get right to the point. I'm taking you as my wife, and I want to know if you're going to live up to that responsibility."

Confusion mixed with surprise. "What are you talking about?"

His features looked pained, and he took a deep breath before he spoke. "If I'm going to stand before the Lord and make you my wife, I want to be sure you're not going to forget your upbringing and run off up North with that city fellow."

The words stung. She would never make a promise she didn't intend to keep.

She looked up into his dark eyes veiled with pain and confusion. How much did he know about her love for Jefferson?

"Nicolas," she said slowly, "when I take my marriage vows, I intend to keep them for life."

"As do I," he said as he abruptly released her hand and turned back toward the house.

&

Wednesday morning when Jefferson arrived at the Breaux home, he found Angeline sitting on the porch, her Bible spread on her lap, and the baby playing on a blanket in the shade at her feet. When he left Latanier, he'd told himself— and Mrs. Mike—that he would merely check in on the recuperating Breaux girls. By the time he turned onto the dirt road that wound alongside the Nouvelle, he had added another purpose to his trip.

Today he would begin the process of courting Angeline Breaux.

All the way from town, he'd planned his course. With less than two weeks before he had to be in New York, he had to act swiftly. Still, he must be wise and gentle and—the enormity of his task was overwhelming.

But, as Pop would say, he was a Villare, and a Villare never gives up.

"Good morning!" he called as he climbed out of the Model A and snatched up his medical bag.

"Jefferson!" Angeline closed her Bible and set it on the porch step. Rising, she scooped the baby onto her hip and strolled toward him. "I didn't expect to see you today."

"So am I a nice surprise?" He tickled the baby under her fat chin and laughed when she giggled.

Angeline's troubled expression caught him off guard. "Of course," she said a bit too quickly. "It's always nice to see you here."

"And it's even nicer to be here." He shook off the feeling that something had changed between them since Monday and proceeded with the first order of business on his agenda. "So, how are our patients?"

"Mathilde is much better. She's been up and around most of the morning."

"No more fainting spells or fever?"

Angeline shook her head. "The fever broke yesterday morning, and it hasn't come back. She's not as strong as she normally is, but she seems steady enough on her feet, and she's had enough energy to help with some of the household work."

"Good. And Amalie?"

"There's been no change, Jefferson. She sleeps much of the time, and she's not lost that fever yet."

"But it hasn't gone any higher, has it?"

"No, but something's just not right with Amalie. I can feel it, but I can't put my finger on it." Angeline shifted the baby to the other hip. "To tell you the truth, if you hadn't come out here today, I probably would have gone to get you tomorrow."

"Not in that pirogue?"

She smiled and glanced down at her hands, now free of bandages but still bearing the bright pink color of her wounds. "If I had to."

"Why, Angeline, I never figured you for a nurse."

Startled, she looked up abruptly. "I'm not."

"Of course you are." Jefferson gave her a smile. "A good nurse not only reports on what she can see, she also reports on what she thinks she might soon see." He swung the bag over his shoulder and turned toward the house. "It's a rare gift. Maybe you should consider nursing as a career, *Ma Chere.*"

"Oh, I couldn't," she said as she fell in step beside him.

He stopped short. "Why not?"

For a moment, he wasn't sure she would answer. When she did, her words surprised him.

"Because I've got something else planned." She turned her attention to the baby, smoothing her dark hair as she walked beside him. "Something besides a career in nursing or anything else."

What could Angeline Breaux possibly have planned for the rest of her life? The whole of her existence was wrapped up in home, family, and the Bayou Nouvelle. How could any of these things add up to a future for someone like her?

The answer hit him all at once, like a bolt from the blue. "You *are* marrying the Arceneaux fellow, aren't you?"

"Angie, *Bebe*, is that Jefferson Villare with you?"

Jeff tore his attention away from Angeline to see Clothilde Breaux rounding the corner of the house. "Yes, Ma'am," he said. "It's me."

"Good morning, Jefferson," she said as she greeted him with a wave of her hand. "Did you come to see to my girls?"

"Yes, Ma'am." He cast a quick glance at Angeline. *All three of them, actually.*

Clothilde reached for the baby and settled her on her hip. "Just you go on inside then, Jefferson. Angie, go with him and help, eh?"

"Yes, Mama."

"You know my girl, she ought to have been a nurse, eh?" She patted Angeline's shoulder. "She keeps good care of her two sisters and still finds time to watch the baby so her mama can get her yard chores done. I don't know what I would do without her."

"All right, Mama," Angeline said, a flush of pink spreading across her cheeks. "Now you're starting to sound like Papa."

"Oh, hush now. I'm just telling the truth." She motioned toward the house. "Get on in there and see to the girls, eh?"

Mathilde met them on the porch with a weak smile. "I thought I heard a commotion out here."

Jeff studied Angeline's younger sister as he walked toward her. Her coloring appeared normal, with no telltale dark smudges beneath her eyes.

"How are you feeling?" he asked as he pressed his palm to her forehead and found it cool to the touch.

"Much better, thanks to you," she said. "You're a wonderful doctor, Jefferson Villare."

"You can thank the Great Physician, Mathilde. I just work for Him."

"Well, however you did it, you managed to cure me in record time." She paused. "With Angie's help, of course."

"Mathilde, come!" Clothilde called. "I need someone to watch the baby while I put these Easter lilies in pots. Jefferson'll be needing to take one back home to Mrs. Mike when he leaves, and we don't want to keep a busy doctor waiting."

The younger Breaux sister offered Jeff a parting smile and headed toward her mother. He watched her as she took the baby in her arms, satisfied that she had made a full recovery.

"Shall we go see Amalie?" When Angeline nodded, Jeff stepped inside the normally boisterous house and stopped short. "It's quiet as a tomb in here. Are the children still with your aunt?"

"Yes, Papa didn't want to take any chances, and Tante Flo didn't want to give them up so quickly. They conspired against Mama to keep the little ones over there one more night. It wasn't easy, but Papa held his ground. I understand he told her he would hide the paddles for the pirogue too if she tried to slip off and fetch them herself."

Jeff walked past the pier glass and caught his reflection. Angeline moved into focus in the mirror, and his breath caught. In the morning light, she looked beautiful, not like the decorated dolls in Boston or the upper crust doctors' daughters in New York, but with a beauty that radiated from within.

Angeline Breaux was incredible. How had he missed something so obvious? What had he ever seen in any other woman?

Why did he feel like dropping his medical bag and kissing her right on the spot?

As much as he would like to do that, her admission—or rather her lack of denial—that she was to wed Arceneaux had certainly put a damper on his plans to court her. *Lord, did I misunderstand Your intentions for us?*

"Like mother, like daughter?" he asked as he forced his mind back to the conversation. "With taking the pirogue out, I mean."

"I have no idea what you're talking about," she said with a mischievous grin. The smile disappeared and worry etched her face. "Jefferson, do you think it will be safe to bring the children back tomorrow? I would hate for one of them to come down with whatever Amalie has. I mean, if it is the influenza, well, I remember what it was like before when—"

"Hush now," he said. "Since Mathilde recovered so quickly, I can't be sure this is influenza. Even if it is, Amalie has not shown herself to have a bad case of it. From what you've said, her symptoms seem to be fever and lethargy."

"What's that?"

"Lethargy? That's the tendency to want to sleep all the time."

"Oh." She nodded. "Yes, she's definitely had the lethargy."

Her use of the word amused him; he paused to reach for the door to the back bedroom.

"So you're sure about the children coming home tomorrow, then? It's not too soon?"

"Waiting to return until tomorrow is probably best, but I don't see the need to delay them past then." He wrapped his arm around her shoulder and gave her a quick hug. "Don't worry, Angeline. I'm sure Amalie's condition will be fine by then."

He released her to see to the task at hand, that of checking what he expected to be a recuperating Amalie Breaux.

"You really think she will be all right, Jefferson?"

Oh, but he wanted to kiss away the worry on that beautiful face!

Lord, there's hope for the two of us yet, isn't there? Ignoring all caution, he touched her cheek with the back of his hand. "As I told you, I believe she will be fine."

But when he opened the door, he realized Amalie's condition was anything but fine. Even from where he stood, he could see that the little girl had taken a dangerous turn for the worse.

sixteen

"What's wrong?" Angeline followed Jefferson into the room. "Has something happened to Amalie?"

Jefferson's form hid the little girl as he leaned over to examine her. From the way his shoulders slumped, she knew the diagnosis was not good. Rather than answer her question, he reached for his medical bag and pulled out an instrument. As he listened to the little girl's chest, he frowned.

"What is it?"

"How long has she been like this?"

"Like what?"

When he leaned back, Amalie came into view. Her face had gone pale and her breathing seemed shallow and choppy, like she'd run a long way and found it hard to catch her breath. Dark hair curled in damp tendrils around her forehead, and her fingers clutched at the sheet as if she were looking to feel for something that was not there. Worse, Angeline could hear the rattle in her sister's tiny chest.

"I peeked in on her after breakfast, and she was sleeping. I thought she was fine."

She drew nearer and grasped one of her sister's hands. It felt cold despite the warmth of the room.

"How long ago?" he asked as he retrieved his notebook and pencil. "An hour or two, or was it longer?"

Angeline tried to calm her racing thoughts. "I suppose it was around seven, so that would make it two hours ago. Why is she making that sound, Jefferson? It is awful."

He looked up from his writing to meet her gaze. "I won't lie to you, Angeline. Your sister's very ill. What you're hearing is fluid in her lungs."

"That's bad, isn't it?"

"If we can't arrest the process, she could drown in her own fluids."

Terror gripped her. Little Amalie couldn't possibly die!

"It hurts," her sister whispered.

"Where does it hurt?" Angeline watched as Amalie made a weak gesture to her throat and her chest. A second later, she allowed her hand to fall limp at her side. She closed her eyes.

"Amalie, can you hear me? It's Jeff. Remember me? I'm your sister Angeline's friend." He paused to shake her gently. "Wake up and look at me."

Jefferson adjusted Amalie's body to a more upright position, piling the pillows behind her. Rather than remain where he placed her, the little girl began to fight, first lashing out with clenched fists and then twisting her body out of his grasp.

"Help me, please," he said as he clutched at her tiny shoulders. "We need her to sit up."

Angeline stood there, helpless. "What do you want me to do?"

Amalie went stock-still. Her gaze roamed about the room, focusing on nothing in particular.

"Should I go get Mama or Mathilde?"

"No, not yet. I'd rather we stabilize her first. Besides, neither of them needs to be in close proximity to her. Mathilde's too weak, and your mother's with child. I don't want either of them exposed to Amalie should she prove to be contagious." He paused and gave Angeline a direct look. "For that matter, I would prefer if you'd exercise caution while you're near her. Take care to wash your hands and practice good sickroom hygiene. It will keep you healthy."

"I will."

"Good." He turned his attention back to Amalie. "Why don't you talk to her?"

Her brain went numb as Amalie went into action again, kicking and shaking her head as if she didn't recognize her visitors.

"Talk?" Angeline asked. "Do you think that will help?"

"Yes," he said as he ducked a tiny swinging fist. "I need you to calm her down so I can get her into a better position."

Angeline squeezed past Jefferson to reach for her sister. "Amalie, Honey, it's Angie. Open your eyes."

When the little girl didn't respond, Angeline looked to Jefferson for guidance. "Try again," he said as he continued to wrestle with the pillows.

"Amalie! Wake up!" No response. "Amalie Patrice Breaux, if you don't wake up this instant, I'm going to go fetch Mama and Mathilde, and they're going to make you take a nap with the babies instead of swimming this afternoon. Do you hear me?"

This time her sister's eyes opened slightly. "Swimming?" she asked. "I get to go swimming?"

Angeline pasted on a smile. "Yes, Honey, just as soon as Jefferson says you're feeling up to it."

"You mean it?"

Her dark eyes focused on Angeline, then she quickly shifted her attention to Jefferson. Before she could speak, she began to cough, and Jefferson covered her mouth with his handkerchief. When he pulled it away, dark rust-colored flecks decorated the white material.

"Blood?" she whispered as Jefferson nodded his agreement.

"I'm afraid she's developed pneumonia."

"I want to go swimming," Amalie said before going limp in Jefferson's arms.

Angeline worked alongside Jefferson to position her sister as if she were sitting up. When the last pillow had been put into place, she turned to him. "Is there any hope?"

"We can still save her, Angeline," he said as he reached into his bag to remove a stethoscope. "Or rather, God can save her, with our help."

She sank down on the bed and rested her hands in her lap. "How?"

"Let me examine her, and then we'll talk about what to do."

"Can I help?"

He offered a weak smile. "I could use a good nurse right now."

"Well, I don't know how good I am, but I can learn. Just tell me what to do."

As Jefferson took care to check Amalie over, Angeline followed his instructions and assisted him. She lifted her sister when asked and held her hand when she complained. Once, she even caught the little girl before she attempted to climb past Jefferson and head for the door.

That action took the last of Amalie's strength, however. By the time Jefferson finished his exam and made his notes, she was sound asleep, her slumber only interrupted by the occasional fit of ragged coughing.

Angeline fussed with the covers, adjusting them so they were smooth and straight again. Amalie would never notice the effort and would most likely mess them up again before she awoke. Still it made her feel like she'd done something— anything—to make the little girl more comfortable.

"It's as I expected. Her condition has deteriorated into pneumonia." He lifted Amalie's wrist and took her pulse again. "Now that she's worn herself out, her vitals are returning to a more stable rate, but I'm still skeptical as to how well she will do over the rest of today."

"What do you mean?"

"I mean that this kind of condition can cause a patient to

deteriorate rapidly." His gaze met hers. "You said she looked fine a couple of hours ago, right?"

"Yes."

"Well, take the amount of change you see between the state she was in after breakfast and her condition now. As her condition worsens, she will deteriorate even faster."

Angeline stifled a gasp. "You can't let that happen, Jefferson. There must be some way to make her well again."

"Actually, the only way to begin her healing is to empty the lungs of their fluid. For that, I can only recommend one course of treatment." He scribbled one last note on his pad and looked up. "Your sister needs to be in a hospital."

"A hospital?" She shook her head. "We're just poor folks, Jefferson. We can't afford a hospital."

"But the ideal conditions for treating this type of pneumonia are constant care, and the only place she can get that is in a hospital environment." He paused. "There are plenty of people there who are skilled in this sort of illness, and they could give her excellent care."

"We just can't."

Angeline stroked her sister's forehead and fought off panic. Influenza and pneumonia took the elderly and the weak. Amalie was neither, but she had been sick for nearly a week.

She watched Amalie struggle for a breath, then held the handkerchief against her lips when she coughed. Again the cloth came away spotted with blood.

Something had to be done.

Please, Lord, don't let my little sister die. Please fix her and quick.

"*Ma Chere,* you have to take her to the hospital."

His tone was insistent yet gentle and sympathetic. She knew that, even as he said the words, he realized the impossibility of the situation. People like them didn't take their sick to places like that. Unlike Doc Broussard, hospitals didn't take their fees in fish or furs or some other type of bayou produce.

They wanted cash money, something the Breaux family, like too many others on the bayou, had little of. No, there had to be another way.

"Papa can barely feed us all as it is, and there's another little Breaux coming in a few months. All we've got saved will go to paying medical bills once Mama's time comes." She paused to collect her emotions. "Isn't there any other way?"

His silence, combined with the look of sorrow on his face, landed a blow that nearly caused her to double over in pain. Angeline felt a sob well in her throat, and tears stung her eyes.

"You have to do something. Please don't let her die," she whispered.

"Angeline, I. . ." His voice fell away, leaving the anguish in his eyes. "I'm a researcher, not a general practitioner."

"So what's the difference?" she demanded.

"I work with data and lab personnel, not with patients." His shoulders sagged. "You need Doc here, not me. He's the family practitioner."

"You're a doctor. You graduated with honors, so you know medicine, right?" When he nodded, she continued. "And you know about influenza and pneumonia, right?"

"Right," he said softly.

"Then if you know all of this, why can't you just use what you know on my sister?"

He seemed to consider the question a moment. "There were techniques we used in school that might work. We can try and simulate the hospital treatments here," he said slowly. "But I can't guarantee. . ."

"Only the Lord can make guarantees, Jefferson. Just tell me what you need me to do."

"First we need to elevate the bed. Can you get something to put beneath the headboard that will lift it higher?"

Angeline raced to the shed and came back with two bricks, left over items from when Papa repaired the chimney last fall.

While Jefferson lifted the headboard, Angeline slid the bricks into place.

"Now what?" she asked as she climbed to her feet and dusted off her hands.

"Now we work on getting her lungs clear. Follow my lead and do what I tell you, all right?"

When she nodded and moved closer, they set to work. Half an hour later, they had pushed and pounded the poor little girl's back and chest until Angeline thought her sister would never survive the treatment that was supposed to save her. To her surprise, the chest percussion, as Jefferson called it, seemed to help.

Jefferson had patiently instructed Angeline as he went through the motions of the chest percussion. As a result, the muscles in Angeline's arms and back screamed from the exertion.

At least Amalie now lay more comfortably, her breathing a little more even and her cough subdued. Exhausted from the ordeal, however, it was all Angeline could do not to crawl up next to her sleeping sister and fall into a deep sleep.

"Well done, Nurse Breaux." Jefferson tossed a smile in her direction as he put away his notebook and set his medical bag on the nightstand. "I think we just might have caught this thing in time to beat it."

"Thanks to you, Dr. Villare. You're really good at what you do, did you know that?" When he smiled, she felt bold enough to continue. "Are you sure God hasn't called you to be a. . .what did you call it?" She searched her mind for the word he had used. "A family practitioner?"

His expression of surprise startled her. "Do you think you'll be able to do this next time on your own?"

"I'll do my best," she replied.

"Good," Jefferson said as he rose. "I'm counting on my nurse now."

Angeline nodded weakly and gave him a mock salute. "Nurse Breaux reporting for duty," she said with what she hoped would be enthusiasm.

Evidently her words fooled Jefferson, for he looked relieved. He reached for her hand and helped her stand, cradling her against his shoulder when she wobbled on unsteady feet.

"Are you sure you can do this, *Ma Chere?*"

To keep her little sister out of the hospital, she would do whatever it took. She looked up and smiled. "Of course. How often should I repeat the procedure?"

"You'll know when she's in need of a treatment, but as a guess I'd say at least once every two hours for the first twenty-four hours or so. After that, you can probably get away with going three to four hours in between treatments, unless her symptoms worsen. Regardless, someone will have to be with her constantly to monitor her vitals and see that she doesn't take a turn for the worse. Her fever may go up, and that is to be expected. Let me know if it doesn't break and go away completely by tomorrow afternoon."

"I will," she said softly. "Is there anything else I need to know?"

Jeff smiled and collected her into an embrace. "Yes, that I'll be praying for your sister and for you."

Too soon he released her and made his exit. "Every two hours," she whispered as she rubbed her tired arms and watched the motorcar disappear in a cloud of dust. *Father, You and I are going to have to do this together. I know I can't manage it alone.*

Too many hours later, Angeline slumped back in the little straight-backed chair and tried to close her eyes. The morning sun now filtered through the partially closed shutters and fell in long stripes across the floor, casting the room in an odd combination of light and shadows. In the light, Angeline watched her sleeping sister. Amalie slumbered peacefully.

The night had been a long one, and her only rest had come when Ernest and Papa took over for a few hours each so she could curl up in the empty bed. Her sleep had been fitful, filled with dreams of awakening to find Amalie dead.

It had been nearly impossible to keep Mama out of the room. Finally, when Papa threatened to take her to Tante Flo's right then if she didn't remove herself from the doorway and get some sleep, she grudgingly gave in and went to bed. Mathilde had been easier to convince. Her strength had not yet returned completely, so she could do nothing but see that the washbasin stayed filled with cool water. Finally, after midnight, she'd grown weary of even that small job and pleaded exhaustion.

With each treatment, Amalie seemed to breathe easier, and sometime before daybreak her coughing had all but disappeared. Still the fever, which had spiked dangerously high as Jefferson predicted, failed to break.

Angeline rose and stretched the kinks out of her spine. Trudging over to the washbasin, she took a clean folded towel and dampened it. The little girl's eyes opened when the towel touched her skin but soon closed again.

She looked much better this morning, and the color had begun to return to her skin. A glance at the clock on the nightstand told Angeline another hour stood between her and the time for a treatment.

Outside she heard the sound of Papa and Ernest at work on their chores, and she could smell bacon frying in the summer kitchen. Her stomach protested its emptiness, but her legs refused to carry her any farther than the empty bed. With a sigh, she placed her head on the pillow and took one last look at Amalie.

"I'll just close my eyes for a minute," she whispered. "If you need me, you call me, Amalie."

"I will, Angie," she thought she heard her sister say.

The next voice she noticed belonged to Jefferson. "Hush now, we don't want to wake her," he said.

"The poor girl, she's exhausted," she heard Papa say.

"Tried to save her on her own," Ernest added.

When she opened her eyes, none of them were there. Angeline sat up with a start and almost knocked the clock off the nightstand reaching for it. Four hours had passed since the moment she'd placed her head on the pillow.

"Oh no, it's almost noon and I've missed her treatment!" she said as she threw back the blanket and climbed over to Amalie's bed.

It was empty.

seventeen

Jeff stood over the sleeping form of Amalie Breaux and gave thanks to God that he had obeyed the nudging in his spirit that morning. While he had meant to spend the day preparing to leave, he'd felt the strongest urge to head for the Breaux home.

He'd known he would end up there before nightfall, both on the obvious premise of checking on Amalie and the more secret one of seeing Angeline, but he hadn't realized he would be led there to save the little girl's life. How like God that He would arrange things in such a way.

When he arrived, Amalie's fever was at a dangerous level. Thanks to Angeline and the breathing treatments, the girl's lungs were clear. This alone had kept her alive until help arrived. Now that she'd received treatment to combat the infection, her vitals were already looking better. When she awakened and asked about Angeline, Jeff knew she was on the mend.

His thoughts turned from the little girl in the bed to Angeline. She'd been exhausted, too tired even to remember that he'd tried to awaken her.

"Where is she?"

Jeff whirled around to see Angeline racing down the aisle of the children's ward. "Over here," he called.

She caught his arm and peered down at her sister, her breath coming in ragged spurts. "How is Amalie?"

"Calm down, Angeline. Your sister's resting comfortably now."

"What happened? All Ernest would tell me is that you came and took her to the hospital. I saw Papa and Mama in the waiting room, and they couldn't tell me anything either. She almost died because of me, and I intend to have some answers."

Fear shone in her wide brown eyes, and it took all the control Jefferson had not to gather her into his arms and kiss the emotion away. Instead, he took a deep breath and let it out slowly.

"I came out to see about Amalie this morning and found her condition had worsened," he said. "Her fever had spiked too high for home treatment, so I brought her here."

Alarm seemed to turn to anger as Angeline's fingers clenched into fists. "Why didn't you wake me up?"

Amalie began to stir, so Jeff led Angeline away from the bed toward the bank of windows. "I tried, Angeline. You were exhausted." He gave her what he hoped would be a stern look. "The last thing your mother needs to worry about is another sick child, namely you. Since you elected not to heed your need for sleep, I made the decision for you."

"But how dare you bring her here to the hospital?" She lowered her voice a notch. "You know Papa can't afford this."

"It's all been taken care of."

Angeline whirled around to see Doc Broussard standing a few feet away. "That is, if you agree to the terms," he added with a wink.

"Terms?" She glanced over her shoulder at Jeff, then returned her gaze to the elderly doctor. "What terms?"

Doc smiled and linked arms with Angeline, leading her past Jeff toward Amalie. Jeff fell in step behind them.

"Well," Doc said, "you know back in 1925, the good people on the hospital board saw fit to name this children's ward after my dear departed wife, God rest her soul."

She nodded.

The old doctor chuckled. "As such, I have a little bit of pull around here." He paused to release Angeline's arm. "So in the Acadian way, I'd like to make a deal, eh? To maybe barter something in return for something else—in this case your sister's hospital bill for something much more valuable that *you* can give to *me*."

When Angeline gave him a perplexed look, he continued. "You know how much I love that shrimp gumbo of yours, don't you?"

A smile dawned on Angeline's face. "Yes, I do," she said softly.

"Then would you consider it a fair trade if I took payment in gumbo? Say one pot of gumbo for each day your sister spends in this fine establishment?" Doc offered a mock frown. "Now I would expect we make this all legal-like. You know, draw out the terms and have both parties sign them. I'm thinking one pot every other Tuesday until the debt is satisfied would do the trick. How does that suit you?"

From where he stood, Jeff could see tears collect in Angeline's eyes. "That would suit me just fine, Sir," she said in a trembling voice.

Doc held out his hand to shake Angeline's. "Good, it's a deal." Abruptly he slapped his forehead. "Wait," he said. "We need a witness." He turned to Jeff. "Come on over here and witness this, would you, Dr. Villare? I wouldn't want this young lady to skip town until her debt is paid."

Jeff closed the distance between them and smiled. "I'd be delighted," he said.

As soon as the words fell from his lips, he wanted to reel them back in. How could he promise to stick around and be sure Angeline brought gumbo to Doc when he planned to be on the train to New York in eleven days?

Surely Doc knew that. Jeff cast a sideways glance at the old man and frowned. The grin on the crafty physician's face told Jeff that Doc knew exactly what he was doing.

No matter. It was all in fun anyway. Angeline would make

a few pots of gumbo, and Doc would beg off the rest of the debt in some polite but subtle way. By then, he would be long gone.

"Jefferson," Angeline said, "I would like to stay with her if I may." She pointed to a pair of chairs next to the ward door. "All I need is one of those to sit in, and I'll be fine."

"Well, I don't know," Jeff said. "Generally the rules are pretty strict about visitors."

He cringed as Angeline's dark brown eyes flashed a pleading glance. "I'm not a visitor. I'm her sister."

He looked to Doc for help. "Still, I don't think it would be allowed, would it, Doc?"

She turned to Doc and touched his sleeve with her fingertips. "Jeff taught me how to do chest percussion, and he says I'm a very good nurse. I could be of help to the staff."

The old doctor smiled. "Is this true, Dr. Villare?"

Ten minutes later, after securing permission, Angeline sat in a soft chair next to Amalie's bed. "Promise me you'll stay out of the nurse's way." Doc motioned to the ward nurse, a friendly woman of middle age, with mock fear. "She's a tyrant, so mind your manners."

"I heard that, Doctor," the nurse called.

"I'll come back to check on the two of you in the morning," Jeff said as he gave Angeline a quick embrace and followed Doc out of the ward.

Instead of waiting until morning, however, he returned to the ward with a hamper of Mrs. Mike's fried chicken and buttermilk biscuits and a tin of fresh field peas in the front seat of the Model A. Anticipation rode high in his mind as he took the stairs two at a time and emerged at the entrance to the Bessie Landry Broussard Memorial Children's Ward.

As he pushed open the big door, he heard laughter inside. What he saw astounded him. Rows of children sat in rapt attention, some in wheelchairs and some propped up in beds, as Angeline told the story of a little alligator named T-Boy and his friend the red snapper. Amalie managed a smile in his direction. The girl looked pale but seemed much improved.

Sinking to his knees behind a little girl in a wheelchair, Jeff held his finger to his lips to tell Amalie he wished to remain hidden. When the little girl nodded and smiled, Jeff turned his attention back to watch Angeline perform each of the voices and act out parts with hand motions.

He looked around at the smiling faces of children who, on every other occasion, wore their illness with stoic silence. Even the ward nurse seemed to be caught up in the tale. When the end came and the unlikely pair lived happily ever after, the storyteller received a hearty round of applause.

Jeff rose to clap the loudest. "Bravo," he called.

Angeline placed her hand over her mouth in surprise. "Jefferson, I didn't know you were here," she said. "How much did you hear?"

"Actually, I think I missed the beginning of the story." He linked arms with Angeline. "Would you kids mind if I borrowed Miss Breaux so she could fill me in on what caused T-Boy and Redfish to go swimming in the first place?"

A chorus of giggles followed them out into the hall and chased them downstairs. When he walked with her into the evening twilight and led her to the Model A, she stopped short and pulled out of his grasp.

"Where do you think we're going?" Her frown did nothing to detract from her beauty. "I'm not leaving her, so if you think you're taking me home, you're mistaken."

Jeff opened the car door and removed the hamper with a flourish. "Relax, *Ma Chere,*" he said. "I bring greetings from Mrs. Mike. Come on. I know just the place to enjoy this bounteous feast."

Her smile restored, Angeline fell in step beside him. "You're the best, Jefferson."

"No, you are. I mean, the way you told that story, it was incredible." He glanced in her direction. "As long as I've been visiting the ward, I don't think I've ever seen those kids smile."

She looked away, clearly embarrassed. "It was nothing."

"Mais non, Ma Chere," Jeff said. "It was definitely something." He nudged her with his elbow. "Let's go that way."

Together, they took the brick walkway toward Community Park. In the center of the park, the white wooden gazebo stood like a beacon, lit by a single streetlight. The night was warm, but not oppressively so, and the breeze smelled fresh with the promise of rain. The ring around the moon confirmed the impending shower.

In a few weeks, band concerts would fill the park with happy sounds, but tonight the music came from the crickets. It was a symphony that strangely suited Jeff tonight, and as he filled his plate with Mrs. Mike's delicacies, he felt nothing but peace.

Tomorrow, he would think about leaving, about his career, and about what God intended for him. Maybe he would even think about Angeline and the fact that she'd been promised to another. She hadn't actually come out and admitted it to him, but the look on her face when he asked her told the tale. Yes, he just might think about that tomorrow.

Tonight, though, his only worry was saving room for peach pie. At least he thought that was his only concern until Angeline surprised him with a question.

"Jefferson, have you ever thought that maybe you misunderstood what God wanted you to do with your life?" She dabbed at the corner of her mouth with a blue-checked napkin, then allowed the folded cloth to drop into her lap.

"I mean, have you ever made up your mind that the Lord had something for you, only to find out He didn't want that for you at all?"

Jeff stalled for time by pretending to chew his food a bit longer than necessary. When he finally swallowed, he could tell by the look on Angeline's face that his ploy had not worked.

"Sure," he said as he expelled a long breath. "I think that happens to everyone eventually. Why do you ask?"

"No reason, I don't guess."

Her voice told him she had plenty of reasons, but logic warned him not to ask. Instead, he went back to his chicken leg, which no longer held any taste. Eventually he tossed it into the woods and leaned back on his elbows.

While they ate, the sky had faded from blue to purple and finally to black. Now tiny stars danced at the edge of the streetlight's glow.

"You're marrying Nicolas Arceneaux, aren't you?" he said, surprising himself with his boldness.

Silence fell between them for what felt like an eternity. Finally, Angeline spoke. "Yes. In ten days."

"Do you love him?" *Where had that come from?*

"Sa fait pas rien," she whispered.

Jeff leaned forward to place his hands on her shoulders. "It *does* matter, Angeline."

"We should go," she said softly. "Amalie will be wondering where I am."

At that moment, he wanted nothing more than to hold her in his arms and tell her she could marry him instead of the big fisherman. Instead, he released her and nodded, packing up the hamper without comment.

If she wants to marry another, who am I to stop her? I've done her a favor in not pressing my case with her.

But all the way back to the hospital's front entrance,

where he allowed her to slip back inside with only the blandest of parting words, he had the awful suspicion that he'd done neither of them any favors.

eighteen

Nine days later, Amalie went home in Jefferson's motorcar with Angeline huddled next to her. She'd barely left the little girl's side, leaving the hospital only to accompany Mrs. Mike back to the Villare house for a hot meal and a change of clothes.

Jeff continued his habit of stopping by to check on Amalie, but he never took Angeline to the park for another picnic. When Mrs. Mike started coming by in the evenings, she saw even less of Jefferson.

It was as if their evening in the park had been a good-bye dinner between friends. Everything else seemed to take place between strangers.

The third day of Amalie's stay, Mama declared the wedding must be postponed. She could not plan a marriage ceremony for one of her girls while another of them was ill, and Reverend Dautrive agreed. Eventually Mama convinced Papa, and the date of the nuptials was erased from the church calendar. The date would be rescheduled soon, Mama promised. In the meantime, all her efforts had to go toward restoring Amalie to perfect health.

Angeline smiled as she recalled the conversation, remembering the twinkle in Mama's eyes when she spoke to Papa. Poor Papa never knew what hit him when Mama went to work on changing his mind. He always thought it was his idea, and Mama always let him.

Yes, her mother was a wise woman.

Thankfully, Angeline was spared having to speak to Nicolas during this time, although Mathilde gleefully informed her that her groom-to-be had taken the news of the postponement in stride. He hadn't said much, according to her sister, but rather listened to Mama's explanation without expression.

The car pulled to a halt in front of the house, and Jefferson got out to fetch Amalie inside.

"I don't want to take a nap," Amalie said as Jefferson placed her on her bed and pulled the covers over her legs.

"What if I promise to tell you a new story about T-Boy once you take a short nap?" Angeline said. "How would that be?"

When Amalie began to argue, Angeline held up her hand. "I'm not going to change my mind. Do you want me to call Mama or Mathilde in here?"

"No," she said as she stuck out her lip to pout.

"Then to sleep with you. Besides, I need some time to think of a new story. You wouldn't want me to tell just any old tale, would you?"

"No," Amalie whispered as she settled her head on the pillows. "Can we still go swimming?"

"No swimming, Little One," Jefferson said, "but what if I come see you in a few days and take you fishing? How would that be?"

"Fishing? Oh, I suppose so."

"Good, then mind your sister and get some rest."

"But I'm not tired," she said as she pulled the blanket up to her chin. Exhausted from the trip, however, Amalie easily slipped into slumber within minutes.

Jefferson took one last reading of the sleeping girl's vitals, wrote them on his tablet, and then rose. Angeline followed him outside, listening while he fended off Mama's questions.

"I'm sure she's perfectly fine," he said for the second time. "She's a little weak from all she's been through, but she's definitely on the mend."

"And I won't catch nothing from her now?"

"You'll be fine," he called as Mama brushed past him to

disappear into the room where Amalie slept.

"That's probably the last we'll see of her tonight," Angeline said. "Papa says she's driven herself to distraction worrying about Amalie and not being able to take care of her."

"What's that you say about your papa?"

Angeline looked up to see her father standing in the door. "I was just telling Jefferson how Mama's missed being able to take care of Amalie."

Rather than comment, Papa crossed the room to stand toe-to-toe with Jefferson. "I heard tell down at the post office that you're leaving tomorrow on the morning train."

The statement hit Angeline square in the heart. Jefferson had said nothing about leaving tomorrow. While she'd kept quiet about the postponement of her wedding, she'd secretly hoped that he knew and would soon step in to declare his feelings.

What she would do if he did, she hadn't decided. After all, there was the not-so-small matter of Papa and Nicolas Arceneaux.

"What's the matter, Boy? Cat got your tongue?"

"No, Sir." Jefferson squared his shoulders and stared down at Papa. "Actually, that's old news."

"Is it now?" Papa crossed his arms over his chest and frowned. "Then why don't you just give us the latest report?"

"Actually, I've been so busy helping Doc, what with the influenza outbreak, that I secured permission for another month's vacation." He locked gazes with Angeline. "I leave for my research position in New York on June tenth."

June 10. The day will be here before we know it, Lord. Work fast, please.

Papa took a step back, a stricken expression on his face. "I reckon I ought to thank you for what you did for my little girl. You saved her life, and for that, her mama and me will always be in your debt."

"Actually, it was Angeline who saved her life."

Papa whirled around to face her. "What?"

"She's quite the nurse, Mr. Breaux." He smiled in her direction. "If she hadn't kept the chest percussion up, your daughter would never have withstood the fever when it spiked. I just happened to show up at the right time with the car."

Papa looked at her with admiration she did not feel she deserved. "But I fell asleep," she said. "She almost died because of me."

"That's not true, Angeline," Jefferson replied. "Because of the treatments you gave her during the night, her lungs were almost clear at the time the fever hit her the hardest. One condition had nothing to do with the other. There was nothing you could have done, even if you had been awake."

Relief washed over her. "Really?"

"Really."

That one word held more comfort than Angeline thought possible. All this time, she had worried that her lapse in nursing skills, and the weak moment when she closed her eyes, had nearly cost her sister her life.

"Theo, come see your baby girl," Mama called. "She's awake and asking for her daddy."

Papa stuck his hand out and shook Jefferson's. "I still want to thank you for what you did."

"It was my privilege, Sir," Jefferson said.

Angeline watched as the two men who mattered most in her life embraced. Only God could have brought together these most unlikely of allies.

"You're welcome back here anytime, Villare," Papa said in an unsteady voice as he hurried toward the back bedroom. "There's my little girl," Angeline heard him call as he disappeared inside and closed the door.

"I'll walk you out," Angeline said.

Together they strolled toward the motorcar. "How long

before she's completely well?" she asked when they reached the vehicle.

Jefferson tossed his medical bag on the seat and turned to face her. "Could be days, could be weeks. It's in God's hands now."

"But she's going to be fine, right?"

He nodded. "Of course she is. She's got the best nurse around." Pausing, he leaned against the car door and crossed his arms over his chest. "Still, I may have to come and supervise her care. Just to be sure."

"I would welcome that, Dr. Villare."

What was wrong with her? She was practically married off to Nicolas Arceneaux, and yet here she stood out in broad daylight, flirting like a schoolgirl with Jefferson Villare.

She should stop this nonsense right now; stop believing that God just might make a way for her to have a future with the young doctor instead of the fisherman. If God put the dream in her heart, surely He would make it come true.

"Maybe we can go fishing while I'm here. We haven't done that in a long time. If Amalie's up to it, she can come along."

The statement took her aback. Fishing with Jefferson sounded fine, indeed.

Angeline met his gaze and smiled. "I would like that very much, and I know my sister would too." When he left, the smile remained.

≈

"Who's ready for some fishing?"

Jefferson burst through the door with a smile on his face and a collection of cane poles in his hand. "What's the matter? Am I early?"

Amalie giggled and raced for the door. "Let's go, Angie," she called as she ran past Jefferson to head outside.

He'd worn his fishing clothes this time instead of his usual dapper suit. Funny, how the casual trousers and shirt put her in mind of the young man he had been rather than the grown man he was.

"I see she's recovering nicely," Jefferson said. "No more symptoms?"

"None. That's four days with no fever or cough." She smiled and picked up the basket holding the lunch Mama had packed for them. "And as you can see, her strength has returned."

Jefferson turned to look over his shoulder at the little girl now skipping in circles on the front lawn. "I see that," he said. "In fact, I'm wondering if they gave her too much good care over at the hospital. Maybe you should complain."

Angeline laughed and followed him out the door. As they walked toward the bayou, Amalie lit out ahead of them. By the time they reached a good spot for fishing, she had doubled back and stood in their path.

"You're slow," she said. "Come on!"

Looping the handle of the basket over a low-hanging cypress limb, Angeline settled in a shady spot beside the bayou and watched as Amalie danced in circles. "See, Angie, I'm a princess. A beautiful dancing princess."

"Yes indeed, you are," Angeline said. "But if you're not careful, you'll tire yourself out, and we'll have to go home."

She stopped twirling to put her hands on her hips. "Before I swim?"

Jefferson shook his head. "No swimming today, Young Lady. That would definitely be against doctor's orders."

Amalie frowned and sank down next to Angeline. "But I wanted to go swimming."

"Hush," she said. "Today you're going to fish instead."

"But fishing's no fun."

Jefferson leaned close. "That's what I thought too until I learned to like it. After that, I always caught the biggest fish."

Angeline laughed. "You did not. In fact, if I remember

right, you could barely sit still long enough to catch any fish at all. Generally our fishing competition ended up being a kick-the-water contest instead."

"That sounds like fun," Amalie said. "How do you play kick-the-water, Dr. Jefferson?"

"Oh no, you don't," Angeline said. "Don't show her, Jefferson. She's just looking for an excuse to get wet."

She caught the twinkle in his eyes before he spoke. "Sounds like the voice of experience." He reached for the smallest cane pole and settled down beside Amalie. "Now, watch this." He reached into the fishing creel, pulled out a small tin, and retrieved a red wiggler. Spearing it like a pro, he handed the pole to Amalie. "Now keep your worm in the water and see if the fish are hungry."

"All right," Amalie said as she wrapped her little hands around the end of the pole.

Jefferson nudged Angeline. "Want me to bait one for you?"

"I'll just watch for now," she said.

A few minutes later, the little girl had tired of the activity, leaving Jefferson to take over her pole. While Amalie chased a butterfly, Angeline chased memories.

❧

How many times had the two of them made the trip down to the bayou, promising to bring home fish for dinner but returning with nothing but soggy clothing and an afternoon wasted on fun?

Oh, but those were the days.

"A penny for your thoughts," Jefferson said.

For a moment, she considered not answering him, then she thought better of it. "I was just thinking about how much fun we used to have here." She paused. "Before life made grown-ups of us."

"I think about that a lot." He stuck the end of the cane pole in the soft ground and leaned back on his elbows.

"Thinking about you is what got me through the first year away from home."

His statement took her by surprise. Rather than respond, she tried to hide her feelings by pretending to study the dark water of the bayou as it flowed past.

"Did you ever think about me, Angeline?" Out of the corner of her eye, she saw him roll over on his side to face her, cradling his head in his hand. "I mean, did you miss me at all?"

"Miss you?" Angeline shook her head. "That's all I did," she whispered. "I missed you until I thought I would never get over it."

"Did you?" He paused. "Get over it, I mean?"

"No." Angeline met his gaze. "Every day I expected I would look up from my chores and there you would be, standing on the other side of the bayou, looking like you'd never left."

"And then one day, I was."

She nodded.

"But I was too late."

The truth of that statement stung. Had he arrived even a week before, maybe Papa wouldn't have made plans to marry her off to Nicolas Arceneaux.

No, she couldn't be sure of that. Jefferson's return to Bayou Nouvelle could have given Papa enough reason to marry her off, no matter when it happened.

"I don't think you were too late, Jefferson," she said slowly. "I prefer to think that God just had other plans for us."

"Is that what you think?"

His dark eyes bore into her soul and she longed to tell him how she really felt, how she would leave the bayou with him tomorrow if God would only release her to do that. Instead, she held her peace and said, "Yes, it is."

"Are you set on marrying this Arceneaux fellow, then? Do you think that's what God plans for you to do?"

"I think that's what Papa plans for me to do," she said, allowing him to gather what he would from her statement. There was no sense in revealing the details of the humiliating barter deal she'd been a part of. What good would come of him knowing she'd been traded like a pile of furs to the fisherman?

Jefferson leaned toward her. "Do you love him?"

Again, the truth served no purpose, so she decided to say nothing.

Abruptly Jefferson climbed to his feet and reached for her hand. Angeline allowed him to pull her up into a standing position.

"Answer me this, and I will never ask again," he said as he held her hand against his chest. "Is it Arceneaux you love, or could it be me?"

nineteen

Angeline looked away, focusing on her little sister, who skipped happily in circles in the distance. "Don't ask me to answer that."

"I think you just did." With that Jefferson swept her into an embrace. "Oh, *Ma Chere,* we are a pair, aren't we?"

It felt so right to be held in his arms, but she knew it was so wrong. Amalie might notice them and misinterpret their embrace. Or worse, she could see it and understand completely.

Such were the ways of the little ones. They seemed to know things even the grown-ups missed. Perhaps Amalie already knew of her feelings for Jefferson. She certainly went out of her way to mention the man whenever she could. And when Nicolas Arceneaux's name came up, Amalie was the first to offer a frown.

Reluctantly, she pulled away. "God wants me here at Bayou Nouvelle, and He wants you up North. We weren't meant to be, so what does it matter?"

Jefferson took a step toward her, then seemed to think better of it and backed away to place his hands on his hips. "Remember when you asked me if I ever thought I might have misunderstood what God had planned for my life?"

Angeline nodded.

"I could ask you the same thing." He looked past her to the bayou and the cane pole still stuck in the dirt. "Have you ever wondered that?"

Again, she nodded. "Sure."

"How do you know He didn't intend us to be together?"

"I don't," she whispered.

"Then how can you dismiss the possibility?" He caught her into another embrace, and this time he added a kiss on the forehead and another, softer one on the lips. "At least you can acknowledge your feelings for me, can't you?"

No, she meant to say. It came out "Yes" instead.

"Angie. Are you and Dr. Jefferson done with your fishing?"

The sound of her sister's voice broke the moment and the embrace. Angeline stepped away and wrapped her arms around her waist.

"Maybe we're finished with the fishing," Jefferson said softly, "but we're *not* finished with this conversation." He reached past her for the picnic basket. "And I don't think God's finished with us either."

Angeline continued to think about this statement long after the day had ended. As she went through the motions of completing her household chores and looking after Amalie and the little ones each day, she often revisited the moment on the banks of the Bayou Nouvelle. Someday soon, she would have to put the memory behind her and be a good and faithful wife to Nicolas Arceneaux, but for now she allowed thoughts of Jefferson to entertain her as she hung the freshly washed sheets on the clothesline.

These thoughts fled with the arrival of Reverend Dautrive. "Wonderful news, Angeline," he cried as he unfolded his large frame from the motorcar.

Angeline snapped a clothespin on the end of the last wet sheet and picked up the empty basket. "Hello, Reverend," she called.

"Who's here?" Mama said from inside the house. When she emerged on the porch, she waved. "Hello there, Reverend. What a pleasure to see you today."

The reverend tipped his hat and lumbered toward Mama. "The pleasure is mine, Clothilde. I thought I would stop by and deliver the good news to you ladies personally."

"Good news?" Mama looked toward Angeline, who shrugged.

"There's an opening on the church calendar," he said with a grin. "I can marry Angeline and the Arceneaux boy on. . ." He paused to open his notebook and flip through the pages. "Yes, here we go, June tenth."

June 10. Oh no, not the day Jefferson is set to leave. But that's just a few weeks away.

"That's fine, Reverend," Mama said, ushering him toward the porch. "I'll give Theo the good news when he gets home, and I'll send Ernest down to speak to Nicolas in the morning. Now, can I offer you a glass of sweet tea?"

Angeline dropped the laundry basket and sank to her knees. *Father, if ever there was a time to show Your sovereign will, it is now. Please do something, and quick.*

❧

Jeff had to do something and quick. With June 10 looming large on the desk calendar in Pop's office, he had little time to decide what God wanted him to do. Until his return to Latanier, he'd always been so certain of what he was to make of his life. Now the only certainty in his life was that he was uncertain about everything.

Everything except Angeline Breaux, of course. He knew exactly how he felt about her.

He loved her. That was the problem.

The doorbell shattered his thoughts. Thankful for the interruption, he rose to answer the door before Mrs. Mike could get to it.

"Good to see you, Doc. Come in." He swung the door open wide and gestured for the old man to come inside. "What a pleasant surprise. I thought you were much too busy for house calls these days."

Doc chuckled and removed his hat, depositing it and his medical bag on the credenza. "I am busy, that's true."

"How about a cup of coffee?"

"And I've got a pie fresh from the oven," Mrs. Mike called from the kitchen.

"I'd be delighted," Doc said.

Jeff led the way to the kitchen. "Any new cases of influenza?" he asked over his shoulder.

"One," Doc said as he fell in step behind Jeff. "A young man down at the sawmill fell sick yesterday afternoon. Foreman thought it might be heat exhaustion, but one look at him and I knew that wasn't the trouble." He sank onto the chair and leaned his elbows on the table. "I sure hope he's the last one for awhile, but you never know."

"At least we can be thankful the Lord didn't take a single soul this time around," Mrs. Mike said as she placed dessert plates overflowing with peach pie in front of the men. "Back in 1918 we weren't as blessed." She touched Jeff's shoulder. "God rest your dear departed mother's soul."

He nodded and attempted to swallow the lump in his throat. Finding a cure for the disease that took his mother had consumed his life. Hearing this reminder made him remember how very much he wanted to do that.

He wanted.

Jeff stifled a groan. Had he been so wrapped up in what he wanted that he had decided that's what God wanted too?

"Amen to that, Mrs. Mike," Doc said. "You know, the one thing I don't think I'll ever get used to is losing a patient." He stabbed at the pie with his fork. "Oh, I know there's a much better place they're headed for, but it just seems like the Lord put me here to keep those folks around as long as I can and not to usher them to Jesus."

Mrs. Mike filled Doc's coffee cup with steaming chicory coffee, then poured some for Jeff. "I agree, Doc." She deposited the coffeepot on the table between them along with the sugar bowl and shrugged. "But you can't argue with the Lord's timing. Sometimes He says to stay, and sometimes He says to go."

Those words, simple and yet complex, struck Jeff right to the heart. Yes, sometimes He did.

At that moment, over pie and coffee, Jeff felt God was telling him to stay in Latanier. He watched the housekeeper leave the kitchen with a new respect. Who knew Mrs. Mike was such a philosopher?

"Oh, my goodness, I almost forgot." Doc fished a folded paper from his vest pocket. "This is for you, Jeff. I told Amos down at the telegram office I would deliver it and save him a trip."

Jeff unfolded the telegram and read the words. It was from Columbia University.

Huge breakthrough in pneumococcus research days away. Need full team in place immediately to process data and analyze results. June 10 no longer acceptable arrival date. Come at once.

"Bad news?" Doc asked.

Stunned, Jeff dropped the paper and watched it float to the floor. Doc picked it up and read it.

"Well, well, this is *good* news." He clapped a hand on Jeff's back. "Congratulations, My Boy. Looks like you're about to make history. Your father would be so proud."

"Right," he managed to say through the cotton filling his throat.

Doc pushed back from the table and regarded him with a curious stare. "You don't look so happy. Want to tell me why?"

Jeff expelled a long breath. "I wish I knew."

Doc reached for his coffee cup and took a sip. "That woman makes the best coffee." He set the cup down and gave Jeff a wry smile. "Could it be you're having second thoughts about going to New York?"

"It could be," Jeff said slowly. "Trouble is, I don't know if I'm having a problem with this because *I* want to stay or because *God* wants me to stay." He paused to pick up the telegram and scan it once more. "Until you handed me this, I thought God was telling me to stay."

"So what changed your mind?" He pointed to the paper. "This? It's just a telegram, Jeff, not a message from the Lord."

"How do you know that, Doc? What if it is a message? What if God is telling me I'm supposed to go to Columbia and work on that team? I mean, my goal has always been to do that. I owe it to my mother's memory."

Silence fell between them. Finally, Doc cleared his throat.

"So that's why you were always so all-fired bent on doing research instead of taking over your father's practice." He leaned back in his chair and studied Jeff. "I don't know why I didn't see it before now, but it sure makes sense."

Irritation sparked. "What makes sense?"

"You getting ahead of the Lord, that's what." Doc's eyes narrowed. "Here you are a trained medical doctor who ought to be practicing medicine with real people instead of looking into beakers and microscopes all day." He leaned forward. "You're wanting to even the score over your mama's death by finding a cure, aren't you? That's why you're bound and determined to head off to New York and set the world on fire, instead of staying here and saving lives."

"Am I?"

Jeff tried in vain to conjure up an argument against the ludicrous suggestion. Surely his whole life plan hadn't come from such a simplistic need for revenge over the death of his mother.

Or had it?

"Well, before you cash in that train ticket, let me give you another option." Doc smiled and rubbed his balding head. "I'm an old man, and one of these days I'm not going to be wanting to do all the doctoring I can do now. What with your pop gone and me the only doctor left in town, I've been looking to take on a partner."

He held up his hand to silence Jeff's protest.

"Now before you go saying something you might have to take back, let me just remind you that the job of doctoring the fine people of this parish was good enough for your daddy and your granddaddy, and I hear tell your great-granddaddy did a might of doctoring of his own." He paused and gave Jeff a direct look. "That's a long line of history you're trying to break. You better be sure the Lord's telling you to break it."

"Yes, Sir, I'll give it some serious thought."

Doc nodded and rose. "That's all I ask," he said as he disappeared into the hall.

As the door closed behind the old doctor, Jeff leaned his elbows on the table and rested his head in his hands. All he'd ever dreamed of in the way of a career in biological research now sat within his reach. He toyed with the edge of the telegram and tried to decide what to do.

God had given him the ability to learn medicine and the opportunity to do something valuable for mankind with that knowledge. On the other hand, He had also given him a shot at doing something for the people of Nouvelle parish. Without Doc, and in the absence of any new physician who might be found, they would be forced to take the long ride upstream to New Iberia for medical care.

More important, to stay would be to press his case with Angeline. Until she walked down the aisle with the fisherman, God could still intervene.

The offer to stay was tempting. But was it what God wanted?

Jeff rubbed his face with the palms of his hands. Nothing would be gained by hashing the problem over in his mind.

Seeking asylum in his favorite place, he strolled into Pop's office and sat in the big leather chair. Perhaps something in here would give him the guidance on what to do about his dilemma.

Absently, he opened first one drawer and then another until a glint of gold caught his eye. His mother's wedding ring.

Jeff picked up the delicate band and weighed it in his palm. Had it always been in the desk? He couldn't remember seeing it before now, and he must have gone through the contents of these drawers a half dozen times in his quest to clear the office of Pop's things.

Jeff leaned back in the chair and clutched the ring to his chest. *Lord, is this some sort of message from You?*

Tucking the ring into his vest pocket along with his watch, Jeff headed toward the garage and the Model A. If he hurried, he might be engaged by sunset.

twenty

Angeline stood along the banks of the bayou, wondering if she'd made the biggest mistake of her life. All day she'd prayed and planned, and now, with just a few minutes to go, she began to think better of the whole thing.

What did she think would come of arranging a private meeting with Nicolas Arceneaux just to see if she could really forget her feelings for Jefferson and fall in love with him? Did she actually believe it mattered what her feelings were for him?

Papa declared she would marry that man, and Papa's word was his bond. Nothing, short of the Lord, would keep the wedding from happening.

And that is why she had to see Nicolas today.

Maybe God would speak to her in the quiet of her visit with Nicolas. Maybe He would gift her with the ability to love the man. Or maybe He would guide her once and for all in the way He wanted her to go. Dare she hope it would not be with Nicolas Arceneaux?

A rustling on the trail ahead told her someone was coming. Ernest appeared in the path with Nicolas a step behind.

"I don't know what you're up to, Angie, but if Papa finds out I left my work to fetch Nicolas, he'll have my hide," Ernest said.

She gave her brother a thankful smile. "He won't find out."

"I'll be just over there." Ernest pointed to Papa's workshop in the distance. "Holler if you need me, Angie."

"I will." She offered Nicolas a shy smile. "Thank you for coming to see me, Nicolas. I know it was difficult to leave your work today, and I appreciate that you did."

Nicolas gave her a perplexed look. "I will say I was a little surprised when Ernest came to fetch me this morning and said it was an emergency. I thought something bad had happened."

She shook her head. "No, and I'm sorry you were alarmed. I just needed to talk to you." Frustration caused her to pause. "Actually, that's not exactly right."

Heat flooded her cheeks. This wasn't turning out at all like she planned.

Angeline looked up into the eyes of the fisherman and repeated the prayer she'd been praying for the past week. *Father, if Nicolas is the man You intend for me to marry, give me the heart to love him. Guide me and allow me to be the wife he needs me to be. Most of all, if he's not the one, please let me know.*

"Angeline, I'm confused," Nicolas said. "Why am I here?"

"For this."

With that she boldly wrapped her arms around him and kissed him soundly.

❧

Jeff pulled the motorcar to a halt outside the Breaux home and scanned the property to see if Angeline might be outside. When he didn't see her, he headed for the front door, only to be met by Mathilde.

"Welcome, Jefferson," she said. "What brings you here this afternoon?"

"Actually I came to see Angeline. Is she here?"

"Doctor Jeff!" Amalie came bounding across the room and launched herself toward him, landing in his arms just as he knelt down. "I missed you."

The collision bowled him over, and he landed on his rear. His watch flew out of his pocket and hung by its chain from a vest button.

"I missed you too," he said when he recovered and tucked the timepiece back inside. "You look like you're feeling better than ever."

"Oh, she's perfectly well," Mathilde said. "Unless you're

depending on her to do her chores. Then she suddenly feels ill and can't move a muscle."

Jeff rose to a sitting position. "Is that true, Amalie?"

Amalie shook her head and leaned close. "No, but if it was, you wouldn't tell Mathilde, would you?"

"I think she already knows," Jeff whispered, giving the older Breaux sister a conspiratorial wink before he turned his attention back to Amalie. "Say, you wouldn't happen to know where Angeline is, would you?"

"I do, but I'm not supposed to tell." She lowered her voice a notch. "If Papa finds out, he'll have Ernest's hide. That's what he told Angie before he left."

Mathilde's frown told Jeff she had no idea what Amalie meant. "Are you making up stories?"

Amalie stuck out her lower lip. "No, I'm not making up stories. I was supposed to be taking a nap, except I was sitting by the window playing with Ima Jane. . . ." She turned to Jeff. "That's my doll. Anyway, I was playing with Ima Jane and I saw Ernest and Angie standing over by Papa's shed, and that's what Ernest told her before he left in Papa's old pirogue."

"So where is Angie now?" Mathilde asked.

"I told you I'm not supposed to tell."

Jeff leaned toward Amalie and lowered his voice. "If you tell me where Angie is, I'll see if I can't get Mathilde to ease up on your chores for the rest of the day. What do you say?" He looked up at Mathilde for confirmation, then returned his gaze to Amalie. "Where's your big sister?"

Amalie seemed to consider the proposition a moment. When her smile dawned bright and wide, Jeff knew he'd won.

"C'mon, I'll take you there," she said as she tugged on his hand.

Together they rose and walked out onto the porch. Amalie began to skip across the lawn until she reached the path leading to the bayou. Jeff stopped short and knelt down to get on eye level with Amalie.

"I need to speak to your sister alone. Is that all right with you?"

Slowly she nodded. "I guess so. Will you come see me before you go home?"

"Sure," he said as he patted her on the head and sent her on her way back to the house.

Jeff rose and turned to face the path that led to Angeline. "Lord, if this is meant to be, show me in a way that is clear and obvious. If it's not, make that plain too. Either way, I'll bow to Your desires," he whispered as he stepped onto the path.

With the ring snug in his pocket, Jeff set off toward the bayou. In a few minutes he would see Angeline. What would he say?

Perhaps he should have planned this better. Shouldn't a gentleman make some sort of presentation before actually making the proposal? Times like now, when manly advice was at a premium, he missed Pop the most. Yes, Pop would have known exactly what to say.

"Will you marry me, Angeline?"

He shook his head. Too abrupt.

"Angeline, *Ma Chere,* will you marry me and make me the happiest man on earth?"

No. Too desperate.

Flowers. He should at least have flowers to present. Jeff cast about for something in bloom and found only a smattering of pink buttercups hidden beneath the fronds of a palmetto.

Gathering up a handful, he shook the dirt off the roots and straightened his vest and jacket. Tomorrow he would bring her a proper bouquet, but for now these would have to do.

Now, back to the proposal. When nothing brilliant dawned on him, he decided to depend on the Lord.

"All right, Father, I'm leaving the words up to You," he

said as he pushed past a low-lying limb and stepped into the clearing.

What he saw froze the blood in his veins. He jumped back into the thicket and peered between the greenery to be sure of what he had actually seen.

Standing a few yards away was Angeline Breaux, seemingly deep in conversation with Nicolas Arceneaux. And then she kissed him.

&

Angeline pulled away from Nicolas's embrace and touched her finger to her lips.

Nothing.

She shook her head. Why did she feel nothing? When Jefferson kissed her, she felt fireworks, shooting stars, all at once.

Maybe she should try again.

Braving a glance up at Nicolas, she saw he too looked perplexed. He leaned against the cypress tree and folded his arms over his chest.

"Why did you do that, Angeline?"

"I had to know," she said softly.

"Know?" Nicolas shifted positions. "What did you have to know?"

Angeline sank to the ground and patted the spot beside her. "Would you sit with me a minute?"

Still wearing his confused look, Nicolas complied. Angeline cast a glance over her shoulder and caught Ernest staring in their direction. When she waved, he went back to chopping wood.

"I'm going to be honest with you, Nicolas." She took a deep breath and let it out slowly, praying God would supply her with the right words.

"You still love that doctor, and that kiss told you that you never will feel that way about me."

"Yes."

He nodded. "I understand."

"You do?" She regarded him with surprise. "How so?"

A look of sadness came over his handsome features. "Because as beautiful and kind and sweet as you are, I don't love you either, Angeline. As I told you before, there's someone else who will always hold my heart."

Relief washed over her. "Then it's settled. We can't possibly marry."

She stood to go and he drew her back down beside him. "It's not settled," he said. "My word is my bond, Angeline. I made a deal with your father and I intend to keep it."

Her heart sank. "You're right," she said. "I don't know what I was thinking." She peered up at him through eyes heavy with unshed tears. "Forgive me for trying to shirk my responsibilities. I was wrong."

Nicolas covered her hand with his. "We'll make the best of this, you and I. In time we'll get used to the arrangement. Who knows, maybe even fall in love someday, eh?"

"Yes." Angeline tried to smile. "I suppose after bringing you all this way, the least I can do is ask you to supper."

"Are you cooking?"

When she nodded, he broke into a grin. "One thing I won't have to get used to is your cooking, Angeline."

He stood and offered her a hand to pull her to her feet. Angeline saw Ernest drop his ax and head toward them.

"What will we tell Papa?" she asked.

Nicolas shrugged and stepped over a bunch of buttercups someone left in the path. "We'll tell him I had an urge to visit my intended."

Intended. She tried not to cringe as she gathered the still fresh blossoms in her hand and brought them home to place in water.

Staring at the pink flowers, she realized she must *do* something. Yes, she decided, she would speak to Papa and reason with him. It had to work—it just had to.

Angeline planned her speech as she walked alongside Nicolas to the house. Tonight, after Nicolas was settled upstairs with the boys and Mama busied herself with putting the babies to sleep, she would corner Papa and try to reason with him. The prospect of speaking to her intimidating father on this subject frightened her so badly she could hardly swallow.

The evening dragged on until Angeline thought the men would never stop talking about politics, the weather, and fishing. When the time finally came and she found herself alone with Papa, however, the speech she'd practiced in her mind went out the window.

Her father sat at the kitchen table, his spectacles on the end of his nose and his Bible spread out before him. Lips moving as he read, his dark eyes scanned the twenty-fifth chapter of the Psalms while his index finger kept his place.

Instead of rational words, she began by pleading. "Papa, please don't make me marry Nicolas. I don't love him," she blurted out.

Papa looked up at her over the top of his spectacles, then slowly took them off and placed them on the open Bible. "What did you say?"

Angeline sank down beside him and placed her hand on his knee. "Papa, Nicolas is a fine man, but I don't love him. I can't marry him."

"You can and you will, Angie." His words were hard, but the look in his eyes was soft. "Baby Girl, I don't know what I'm gonna do with you."

"What do you mean? I'm a big help to Mama, and with another baby on the way, she's going to need even more things done. Why, I could take over for all her chores, even the garden, and she wouldn't have to do a thing." She paused to take a breath. "I'll earn my keep, Papa, I promise."

Papa looked away, and when his gaze returned to her, there

were tears in his eyes. He placed his hand on her head and smoothed back her hair. In the lamplight, she thought she saw his lip tremble.

"Angie, you don't have to talk me into keeping you close to home. If I could, I'd keep every one of my girls right here under my roof until I go meet Jesus, my boys too."

"Is she complaining about marrying Nicolas again?"

Angeline looked up to see Mathilde standing silhouetted in the doorway. "Really, Angie, I don't see what you have to nag about. The man's quite a catch."

Papa slammed his fist on the table. "There, you see. Your sister understands. Why don't you?"

"Because I don't love him," she said as tears began to fall in earnest. She turned to glare at Mathilde. "Please, Papa, if Mathilde thinks Nicolas is such a catch, let her marry him. Sell her off like a load of furs instead of me."

"Don't be ridiculous," Papa said as he jammed his spectacles back onto his face. "You're the eldest, the plans are made, and that's final. Come June tenth, you'll marry Nicolas Arceneaux and that's final."

Angeline fled to her darkened room and flung herself on the bed. She should have known the cause was a hopeless one. Obviously, God intended for her to forget she ever knew Jefferson Villare. Well, He would just have to show her how because she certainly had no idea how to begin.

"Angie?"

She inclined her head toward Amalie's voice. "Yes, Honey."

The bed springs protested with a loud squeak as Amalie climbed up beside her. "What's wrong?" the little girl whispered. "Are you crying?"

"I suppose a little."

Amalie snuggled next to her and wrapped her arm around her middle. "Don't cry," she said softly. "I'll give you a present if you'll stop."

"A present?" Angeline sniffed and dried her eyes on the pillowcase. "Oh, Honey, you don't have to give me a present."

She felt Amalie move off the bed and then return. "I think this was supposed to be yours anyway," she said, as she placed something round in Angeline's hand.

Angeline fumbled for the light. "What do you have here?"

Opening her palm, she saw a gold ring with a brilliant ruby stone in the center of a nest of diamonds. It was exquisite and definitely expensive.

"Where in the world did you get this?"

"I think it fell out of Dr. Jeff's pocket," Amalie said, her face all innocence.

"Dr. Jeff? When did you see Dr. Jeff, and why do you think this fell out of his pocket?"

twenty-one

Jeff stood in the circle of light illuminating his childhood bedroom. All his possessions, what little he chose to take, were packed into two suitcases and waiting in the hall downstairs. It would be several hours until the daybreak train for New York arrived, but he'd been up all night packing and saw no need for sleep now.

Better to get this over with, he decided. Shutting the door on his memories, he walked down to Pop's study and took out a sheaf of writing paper from the drawer. With a heavy heart, he penned a note to Mrs. Mike telling her to close the house and leave all Pop's things as they were. Maybe someday he would return. In the meantime, she could continue to draw her pay and have use of her rooms in the house.

It was the least he could do, considering the woman's faithful service to the Villare family. Family. He let out a wry laugh. He had no family. He was it, the last of a long line of Villares, and when the train left for New York, the line would end.

Angeline had made her choice, and with that choice his time in Latanier had ended as well. What good was a bayou doctor with a broken heart? No, it was better to keep away from the complicated matter of doctoring real live people and go about the business of dealing only with test tubes and microscopes.

Shouldering his bags, Jeff took one last look around, then resolutely turned and walked out into the night. Tomorrow, he would be so far away from the bayou that the memories could not find him.

No, that's not right. They will always give chase. Maybe someday I'll let them catch me.

৵

Angeline dressed at first light and stole away from the house before anyone could miss her. Rather than risk Papa missing one of the boats, she set out walking toward town. By the time she arrived on Jefferson's doorstep, she was exhausted.

Worse than her sore feet was her aching heart. Amalie's story of an excited Jefferson heading down the path toward the bayou kept her awake most of the night. There could only be one reason why she never saw him yesterday. He had seen her first.

Her and Nicolas.

She summoned all her strength and pushed on the buzzer. A moment later, Mrs. Mike answered the door.

"Well, well, Miss Angeline," she said with a smile. "Welcome, Child. Come on in."

Angeline followed the housekeeper inside. The big house felt as quiet as a tomb. Inside her skirt pocket, the ring rested.

"I came to see Jefferson. Is he here?"

"I'm sorry," Mrs. Mike said slowly. "He left this morning."

"Left?"

Her look of pity spoke volumes. "Yes, he's off to New York and that fancy new job of his. Didn't you know?"

Angeline squared her shoulders and forced back the tears as she reached into her pocket and produced the ring. "He left this at my house. Could you see that he gets it?"

She fled before Mrs. Mike could answer. With every step she took toward home, she said a prayer that God would allow her to be the wife she should be. As she prayed, however, she also cried.

To her surprise, she returned home that afternoon to find Mathilde sitting behind Papa's shed in the same state. "What's wrong, Mattie?"

Mathilde looked up, surprised. "Nothing," she said as she looked away. "Everything. Oh, it's just more than I can bear."

Angeline sank down beside her and leaned her back against the rough cypress boards of the shed. Pulling her knees to her chest, she wrapped her arms around her legs and closed her eyes. "All right, Sis. Tell me everything."

When she finished, Angeline looked up at Mathilde. "Does he feel the same way?"

"Yes," she said softly. "I'm so sorry, Angie."

Angeline patted her sister's knee. "Don't be sorry," she said with a smile. "This just might be the very thing God meant to happen."

Mathilde swiped at her tears with the back of her hand. "Do you think so?"

"Yes, I think so, now get up and dry your eyes. We've got some work to do." She reached for her sister's hand and pulled her to a standing position. "I've got a plan, but in order for it to work, we have to tell Ernest. Are you willing to do that?"

❧

June 10 dawned bright, and as the little church began to fill with people, Angeline stood in the pastor's study along with Mama and Mathilde.

A bouquet of pink roses from Tante Flo's garden lay tied with a white ribbon atop her great-grandmother Breaux's Bible. Her veil, sewn with love by Mathilde and Amalie, sat beside the Bible. Angeline lifted the flowers to smell their fragrant blossoms.

"Are you nervous, *Bebe?*" Mama asked as she toyed with the edge of Angeline's white veil.

"Just the usual wedding day jitters." She took the veil from Mama and set it atop her head. The layers of beaded satin and tulle were so thick, she could barely see through them. "I'll be fine as soon as the ceremony is over."

"Yes, you will," Mama said. She turned to face Mathilde. "You look more nervous than your sister."

"Don't be silly, Mama," she said.

"Here, Angeline," Mama said. "Let me pin your veil in better, *Bebe*. It's all crooked. My goodness, this thing is heavy. Why'd you use such thick fabric, eh? You are gonna stumble down the aisle, blind as a bat, with all this stuff over your face."

"It'll be fine, Mama," Angeline said.

Mama fluffed the veil back into place. "Now, that's better."

"Shouldn't you go sit down, Mama?" Mathilde asked.

"That's right," Angeline added. "It's nearly time."

Mama stared at both of them for a long moment. "You two, you're not up to something funny, are you?"

It was all Angeline could do not to giggle when her gaze met Mathilde's. "No, Mama," they said in unison.

"Angie, your papa would never forgive you if you ran off on your wedding day, you know that, eh? And besides, the Lord decides who you're gonna marry, and that's that."

"I'm not running off, Mama, I promise, and I know God's in control. Relax."

"Well then, I suppose I'll go join Papa. It's almost time for the service to start." She gave Angeline a sideways glance. "Sure is strange you wanting to walk down the aisle without your papa holding your arm."

Angeline smiled and patted her mother's hand. "Mama, I told you I wanted to see you and Papa waiting down front together. Besides, don't you think Ernest can handle the job of walking his sister down the aisle?"

Mama sighed and bustled out of the small room. Mathilde closed the door and set the lock. "Are you ready?"

"As ready as I will ever be," Angeline said.

A few minutes later, Ernest knocked on the door. "Reverend Dautrive says to fetch you. It's time."

"Just a minute," Mathilde called. She whirled around to gather Angeline into an embrace. "You can't do this," she whispered. "I can't let you."

Angeline held her sister at arm's length. "Have you changed your mind?"

"No."

"Then there's nothing to talk about. Let's go."

When Angeline and Mathilde walked out together ten minutes later, Ernest whistled low. "You're a beautiful bride. Nicolas is going to be pleased."

"I just hope Papa is," Angeline said softly.

❧

Jeff urged the conductor to hurry, fairly flying down the steps before they were securely on the ground at the station. The train had been delayed in Shreveport and again in New Iberia, and the result was he'd arrived in Latanier a full six hours later than he planned.

Even if he'd been on time, he was probably too late. Still, he had to try.

"Hold up there, Young Man," the conductor called. "You didn't get your bags."

"I'll be back for them later," he cried as he raced away toward the center of town and the little church where a wedding should have started ten minutes ago.

A dark Model A that looked suspiciously like Pop's pulled to the curb beside the train station. "Mr. Jeff!"

"Mrs. Mike?" He leaned into the open window. "What are you doing here?"

"You think you can come back here and me not find out? I'm getting you to the church on time—well, almost on time." She motioned for him to open the door. "Now get in and hang on."

When he complied, she handed him an envelope with his name on it. "What's this?"

"Miss Angeline brought it the day you left." She smiled. "God and I have been talking about when you planned to give it back to her."

Jeff opened the envelope to see his mother's ring. "How did she get it?"

Mrs. Mike shrugged and checked her watch. "I don't suppose you have time to ask her that right now." She pulled next to the curb in front of the church. "Now get on inside and stop that wedding."

"Yes, Ma'am." Jeff gave her a mock salute and tucked the ring inside his vest pocket.

"This time make sure it stays in that pocket until you put it on her finger."

"Will do," he called as he took the brick steps two at a time and pushed hard on the church's ancient cypress front doors.

He could hear Reverend Dautrive, but the words he said were not clear. As long as he wasn't pronouncing someone man and wife, he still had time.

At the altar were the bride and groom, the preacher positioned between them. The Acadian held Angeline's hands in his.

"Wait, stop the wedding!" he said as the doors slammed behind him. "Stop, Angeline, you can't marry him. I love you, and I want to stay here in Latanier and take Doc up on his offer of a partnership."

"Well, now, this is highly irregular," the reverend said. "Jeff, do sit down and let me finish this ceremony."

"I can't do that, Reverend." His gaze sought and found Theophile Breaux. "Sir, I have loved your daughter for as long as I can remember. I had to get all the way to New York City to realize I couldn't live without her."

Theophile opened his mouth to say something, but Clothilde put a hand on his arm and shook her head.

"If you would allow me her hand in marriage, I promise you I will never take her away from Latanier."

An eternity passed before Theophile spoke. "Nicolas Arceneaux, what say you on this?"

"I say I want this bride for my own, Sir." He gathered her to his side.

"You have your answer, Son." Theophile returned to his seat. "Go on, Reverend, and marry up those two."

No, Lord, please don't let this happen. You showed me I had to come back for her, now show me Your favor and allow me to marry her.

Reverend Dautrive nodded toward Theophile, then cleared his throat. "Dearly beloved, we are gathered here—"

Desperation washed over him. Right before his eyes, he was losing the love of his life. He raced toward the altar and embraced Angeline.

"Angeline, no! Don't marry him. Marry me."

"Yes, I'll marry you."

The words came from the back of the church. A gasp went up in the crowd as Jeff looked over his shoulder to see Angeline standing behind the last row of pews.

"But, if you're there then. . ." Jeff lifted the veil of the bride to reveal Mathilde standing there. Out of the corner of his eye, he saw Angeline rushing toward him. He met her halfway and collected her into his arms.

"I missed you," he whispered. "Will you really marry me?"

She snuggled her head against the crook of his neck and leaned into his embrace. "I will."

"What in the world is going on?" Theophile shouted. "What do you girls mean by switching places?" He turned to Mama. "Did you know about this?"

Mama shook her head. "No, not this time."

"I love him, Papa," Mathilde said as she linked arms with Nicolas. "And he loves me."

"I fell in love with her the first time I saw her, but I didn't know she felt the same way." Nicolas stepped forward. "I didn't want to marry her like this, but it seemed like the only way."

"But the license," Papa sputtered. "He was supposed to marry Angie, not you."

"We got one, Sir," Nicolas said. "I promise it's all legal."

"And you?" Papa whirled around to stare at Jeff. "You got a license too?"

Jeff smiled. "Not yet, but I have a ring." He produced the ring from his pocket. "If she'll marry me today, we'll get the license tomorrow, I promise."

"Can you do that?" Papa asked the preacher.

Reverend Dautrive pondered the issue a moment. "I suppose I could, but no honeymoon until it's legal, eh?"

"You can be sure of that." Papa stood once more and glared at Jeff. "Not only is the Lord watching you, but so is her papa and you don't want to tangle with either of us, you hear?"

"Yes, Sir," Jeff said as he walked up the aisle with Angeline at his side. "And I promise I won't disappoint you or Him." He leaned toward Angeline and kissed her soundly. "And I won't disappoint you either. *Je t'aime, Ma Chere.*"

"I love you too," she said as she looked past him to Mama and smiled.

Author's Note

Every Louisiana cook has his or her own recipe for gumbo. Often these recipes have no definitive measuring involved but rather go by sight, taste, and experience. While I have attempted to offer a "real" recipe, this is by no means the only way to make authentic Louisiana Shrimp Gumbo.

Angeline Breaux's Shrimp Gumbo

1 cup vegetable oil
1 cup flour
1–2 cups chopped onions
1 tablespoon garlic powder
1–2 teaspoons celery salt
1–2 pounds shrimp, peeled and headed
¼ cup chopped green onions
salt and pepper to taste

Combine flour and oil in large pot, preferably cast iron. Cook over medium heat, stirring constantly for 20 to 30 minutes, until dark brown. Add onions and seasonings and cook, stirring occasionally for 10 to 15 minutes until onions are soft. Add 8 cups water to mixture and blend. Simmer uncovered 1 to 2 hours, stirring occasionally. Add shrimp and cook additional 15 minutes. Stir in green onions and cook 2 to 3 minutes. Serve over rice.

A Letter To Our Readers

Dear Reader:

In order that we might better contribute to your reading enjoyment, we would appreciate your taking a few minutes to respond to the following questions. We welcome your comments and read each form and letter we receive. When completed, please return to the following:

Fiction Editor
Heartsong Presents
PO Box 719
Uhrichsville, Ohio 44683

1. Did you enjoy reading *Bayou Fever* by Kathleen Y'Barbo?
   ❏ Very much! I would like to see more books by this author!
   ❏ Moderately. I would have enjoyed it more if

   _____

   _____

   _____

2. Are you a member of **Heartsong Presents**?   ❏ Yes ❏ No
   If no, where did you purchase this book? _____

   _____

3. How would you rate, on a scale from 1 (poor) to 5 (superior), the cover design? _____

4. On a scale from 1 (poor) to 10 (superior), please rate the following elements.

   ____ Heroine   ____ Plot
   ____ Hero   ____ Inspirational theme
   ____ Setting   ____ Secondary characters

5. These characters were special because?_____

_____

_____

6. How has this book inspired your life?_____

_____

_____

7. What settings would you like to see covered in future
   Heartsong Presents books? _____

_____

_____

8. What are some inspirational themes you would like to see
   treated in future books? _____

_____

_____

9. Would you be interested in reading other **Heartsong
   Presents** titles? ❏ Yes ❏ No

10. Please check your age range:
     ❏ Under 18   ❏ 18-24
     ❏ 25-34   ❏ 35-45
     ❏ 46-55   ❏ Over 55

Name_____

Occupation _____

Address _____

City_____ State_____ Zip_____

TO CATCH
A THIEF

4 stories in 1

*I*n a time when women find career options limited, four Chicago women get the chance of a lifetime—busting a ring of train robbers for the Pinkerton Detective Agency. Working undercover in Windmere Falls, Colorado, they begin to unearth clues overlooked by their male counterparts.

Nobody's expecting much from these female operatives—but breaking the case may take only some womanly intuition and a little faith. Will they ride the rails to success. . .and love?

Contemporary, paperback, 368 pages, 5 ³/₁₆"x 8"

Presents

Great Inspirational Romance at a Great Price!

Heartsong Presents books are inspirational romances in contemporary and historical settings, designed to give you an enjoyable, spirit-lifting reading experience. You can choose wonderfully written titles from some of today's best authors like Peggy Darty, Sally Laity, Tracie Peterson, Colleen L. Reece, Debra White Smith, and many others.

When ordering quantities less than twelve, above titles are $3.25 each.
Not all titles may be available at time of order.

*H*EARTSONG ♥ PRESENTS

Love Stories
Are Rated G!

That's for godly, gratifying, and of course, great! If you love a thrilling love story but don't appreciate the sordidness of some popular paperback romances, **Heartsong Presents** is for you. In fact, **Heartsong Presents** is the premiere inspirational romance book club featuring love stories where Christian faith is the primary ingredient in a marriage relationship.

Sign up today to receive your first set of four, never-before-published Christian romances. Send no money now; you will receive a bill with the first shipment. You may cancel at any time without obligation, and if you aren't completely satisfied with any selection, you may return the books for an immediate refund!

Imagine. . .four new romances every four weeks—two historical, two contemporary—with men and women like you who long to meet the one God has chosen as the love of their lives. . .all for the low price of $10.99 postpaid.

To join, simply complete the coupon below and mail to the address provided. **Heartsong Presents** romances are rated G for another reason: They'll arrive Godspeed!

YES! Sign me up for Heart♥ng!

NEW MEMBERSHIPS WILL BE SHIPPED IMMEDIATELY!
Send no money now. We'll bill you only $10.99 post-paid with your first shipment of four books. Or for faster action, call toll free 1-800-847-8270.

NAME _____

ADDRESS _____

CITY_____STATE_____ ZIP_____

MAIL TO: HEARTSONG PRESENTS, P.O. Box 721, Uhrichsville, Ohio 44683
or visit www.heartsongpresents.com